KEEPING
CHRISTMAS

Two Stories
Two solitary lives
One season of change

WANDA
LUTTRELL

BARBOUR
PUBLISHING

Published by Barbour Publishing, Inc., P.O. Box 719, Uhrichsville, Ohio 44683 www.barbourbooks.com

Our mission is to publish and distribute inspirational products offering exceptional value and biblical encouragement to the masses.

 Member of the
Evangelical Christian
Publishers Association

Printed in the United States of America.
5 4 3 2 1

KEEPING CHRISTMAS

No Holly,
No Ivy

Chapter 1

The bright red cardinals scattered across the snowy branches of the crabapple tree gave it the look of a flocked white Christmas tree decorated with red velvet bows.

"The only Christmas tree I'll have this year!" Loraine vowed. There would be no draping of pine rope or holly, no dragging out of time-honored decorations, no baking, no shopping, no wrapping, no cards. She had absolutely no interest in a traditional Christmas this year. *With no one to share it, why should I?* she thought.

She did enjoy the cardinals, though. In fact, she enjoyed all the little birds that came to the redwood feeder hanging from the crab apple limb just outside the patio fence—the tufted titmice, the juncos, the shy little wrens, even the rascally blue jays that scared away the smaller birds as they swooped down to take over the feeder.

"The crab apple my only Christmas tree and the birds my only Christmas company," she said firmly, pulling on her boots and parka and reaching for the bucket of seed beside the kitchen door. She would spend the usually frantic holiday serenely, alone in the big, old two-story house where she and Jack had raised their three children. *And I will enjoy it!* she thought determinedly as she opened the door and stepped cautiously onto the icy stoop.

The birds' food supply replenished, she went back inside and lit the fire in the kitchen fireplace. Tigger, the plump, old tiger-striped tomcat she let stay in the house for company now that Jack was gone, was stretched out on the couch like he owned the place, already full of milk and his favorite tuna-flavored cat food.

Loraine plumped the pillows on the love seat, refolded the quilted throw, and draped it over the back of the recliner, then looked around for whatever she needed to do next. But the house was neat, vacuumed, and dusted. Both bathrooms were spotless, and the refrigerator and the oven had been cleaned just two days ago.

She took a deep breath and let it out in a long sigh. *Two days before Christmas, and I have nothing to do!* she thought in amazement. *I should be making Susan's favorite potato salad or little Jack's chocolate cake,* she thought. *I should be frantically trying to take in or hem up some new outfit to fit Beth's tiny frame. I should be wrapping stocking stuffers or letting Jack catch me under the mistletoe.*

She pushed away the loneliness that threatened the thin veneer of contentment she had built so carefully. "Nothing to do? Good for me!" she said aloud as she looked around for that John Grisham book she had bought yesterday evening at Wal-Mart. *Skipping Christmas.* It fit her mood perfectly.

Well, she wasn't really skipping Christmas. She had hung a beautiful Douglas fir wreath on the front door and put up both nativity scenes—the traditional one with the stable, shepherds, wise men, and camels, as well as the one with Mary and Joseph, the babe, and anything else she fancied.

Who's to say there weren't birds, geese, mice, a cat, and a sweet little chipmunk nestled in the hay of that stable? And if Saint Nicholas had been there, he certainly would have knelt to worship at the manger, she thought firmly. She looked around for the book, found it, and settled into her recliner.

No, she thought, opening the book, *I won't skip the honoring of the advent of the Savior into the world. I'll be at the midnight service tomorrow night.* Loraine loved the praise and worship, the communion service, the carols, the bells, the candles raised high in recognition of Jesus—the Light—coming into the world at Christmas.

I'm just skipping all the man-made folderol and hoopla that has grown around Christmas, she thought, feeling deliciously rebellious.

It had been a long time since she had wondered what it was that made her children such rebels. She knew it was in their DNA, and most of it, she admitted honestly, didn't come from Jack. She sighed, remembering that rebellion was what got Eve into trouble in the first place. She wanted to be her own god.

Well, I don't want that! she thought. *I'm glad there's Someone up there to direct my steps, as it says in Proverbs 3:5 and 6.* She had tried to live by those verses most of her life, trusting in the Lord, acknowledging him, sharing her faith without forcing it on others. *I try to obey the Lord, and the laws of my country,* she defended herself, *but I do enjoy, on occasion, breaking a musty, old rule or defying some demanding tradition!*

When Jack was still alive and the children were home, she had done it all—weeks of cleaning and sewing, hours of shopping and wrapping, days of baking, all-night cooking before Christmas Eve. Many times, after their family dinner, after Jack and little Jack had gone to bed, she had attended the midnight service. By that time, she was so tired that she often placed Beth on one side of her and Susan on the other to prevent her from falling off the pew if she went to sleep.

This year, Loraine's fourth without Jack, Beth was in Italy, and six-foot-one "little" Jack was somewhere in the Middle East with his army unit. She had sent their cookies and stuffed stockings weeks ago. Susan was visiting her new husband's family in Maine. There were no grandchildren, so she need not slip outside to ring sleigh bells or leave a snack for Santa.

I'll miss the children, she thought, flipping the page in her book. *And I'll miss Jack whether anyone else is here or not. But I'm sure going to enjoy having a hassle-free holiday for the first time in thirty-five years,* she told herself firmly.

"How long has it been since I actually sat down to read a book two days before Christmas?" she asked herself happily.

She was chuckling over the third chapter when the phone's shrill ring cut into her concentration. She picked up the receiver and said, "Hello."

"Merry Christmas!" the cheery voice at the other end sang out. "It's Peggy!"

"Peggy?" Eleanor repeated, unable to keep an edge of displeasure at being interrupted from showing in her tone. "Peggy who?"

"You know," the voice insisted, "Peggy. Down at the Coalition."

Loraine recognized the voice as that of the coordinator of activities down at the Coalition of Committed Christians, where she had volunteered three or four times with some of her church group. She didn't know the woman's last name, barely knew her at all, but she had a sinking feeling that "Peggy" was calling to snatch up some of her peaceful Christmas time.

"I'm calling to see if you could help us out with the Christmas dinner we're serving here at the shelter today at noon. We are holding it on the twenty-third so our people can spend Christmas Eve and Christmas Day with their families. With your family away, I thought you might be free to lend us a hand. I know it's short notice, but I've had three of my servers call in sick this morning."

"I'm sorry," Loraine broke into the woman's spate of words. "I have plans. Maybe some other time. Thanks for calling." She hung up the phone, wondering how this very casual acquaintance had found out about her family being away. *Someone at church must have told her,* she decided.

Loraine tried to settle back into her book, but the mood had been broken. And, to tell the truth, she felt a bit selfish. It would only take a couple of hours, maybe three, from her day, and she still would have this evening, as well as Christmas Eve and Christmas Day, to herself.

Sighing, she closed the book and laid it on the table beside her recliner. Then she found the last number on the caller ID and dialed it.

"Peggy," she said when the woman answered, "I find I can make it after all. When should I be there?"

"Thank God!" Peggy breathed. "As soon as possible. People are already coming in, and it's more than an hour till noon."

"I'll be there in twenty minutes," Loraine promised, hanging up the phone and hurrying to the closet to pull on a Christmassy green sweat suit with a jolly snowman on the shirt. Straightening it up, she noted with satisfaction that it was a little big now that she had lost that last twenty pounds that had weighed her down and plagued her arthritis.

She went into the bathroom and brushed her teeth, ran a comb through her short hair, and lightly touched her lips with lipstick. "Who are you?" she asked the impudent, green-eyed, silver-haired image staring back at her from the mirror. It was a private joke she had developed to keep from being depressed when she encountered more and more evidence of the passing years.

Back in the family room, she perched on the edge of the recliner to pull on ankle socks and walking shoes. She knew from experience that she would be on her feet the entire time she was at the soup kitchen.

"Tigger, I'm going out for a while," she told the cat, rubbing his broad, striped head and scratching a little behind his ears. The cat looked up at her, yawned, and blinked sleepy yellow eyes before tucking his head between his front paws and settling in for a winter's nap. "I can tell you'll miss me!" she laughed wryly, reaching for her coat, wallet, and car keys.

"See you later," she promised both Tigger and John Grisham.

Chapter 2

Loraine eased her small green Honda into one of the few remaining parking spaces, locked the door, and made her way carefully down the sidewalk that had been cleared of snow then dusted lightly by the wind. She certainly didn't want to spend Christmas—or any other time, for that matter—lying in some hospital with a broken bone!

"Thank you for coming!" Peggy greeted her earnestly as she entered the big lobby of the sprawling building that housed both the city's soup kitchen and the Senior Citizens' Center.

"You're welcome," Loraine answered, looking around the room. Already the faux leather couches and chairs were filled with people watching TV, playing checkers, and reading. Many simply stood against the wall, staring at the floor, waiting. Loraine knew that all of them had one thing in common—the desire for a good hot meal. She nodded a general greeting as she followed Peggy's short, stocky figure in tight jeans and bright red sweater to the serving area.

"Honey, am I glad to see you!" Gloria, the head server, exclaimed, a huge white-toothed grin splitting her dark face. "I've only got one other server and two cooks here today, and none of us is an octopus! Here, put on this apron and slap some turkey, dressing, and cranberry sauce on these plates! Oh, and add one of those hot rolls."

Loraine hung her coat on one of the pegs in the hallway and slipped the straps of the big white coverall apron over her neck. She had just finished tying its strings behind her waist when Peggy hollered to the crowd, "Come and get it!"

Slipping on the required latex gloves, Loraine took the first plate from Gloria—already bearing green beans and mashed potatoes—slapped a piece of turkey on it, and added a scoop of dressing and a slice of jellied cranberry sauce. She tossed a hot roll on it and looked up to hand it to the first in line.

The man in front of her reached out stained hands with dirty fingernails to take the plate, his eyes on the food, never meeting hers. Loraine noted that his thin, gray hair straggled over the collar of his oversized Columbo raincoat, and the ripe odor of unwashed flesh wafted through the pleasant aroma of dressing and freshly baked rolls. She held her breath and swallowed hard as he shuffled off to sit at one of the many tables set around the dining room.

Gloria shoved the next plate into Loraine's hands. She glanced up at the woman who took the filled plate from her. The woman's watery eyes were full of gratitude and hunger. Loraine noticed that her worn, dark red coat was fastened across her bony chest with twine. The woman smiled weakly and blinked hard.

"Don't let it get to you, honey," Gloria advised. "Jesus said we would have the poor with us always. Just be glad you're helping feed 'em the only decent meal they get."

Vowing not to look up again, Loraine concentrated on filling plates. Soon her movements became routine— slap a generous slice of turkey on the plate, add a scoop of dressing and a slice of jellied cranberry sauce. Keep your eyes off the pitiful line of humanity winding its way past. Play a game with the round clock on the wall across the room to see how many plates you can fill in five minutes.

"Oh, Mama, it smells so good!" she heard a child exclaim. Involuntarily, she looked up, straight into the sad, tired eyes of a woman standing in line behind three children—a three- or four-year-old boy and two little girls of elementary school age. The children were scrubbed, their hair shiny clean, their mismatched, obviously hand-me-down clothing washed, pressed, and mended. Loraine smiled as the mother and her children passed by, and received an apologetic smile that did not reach the mother's despairing eyes.

What circumstances have caused this woman to seek food from the soup kitchen? Loraine wondered. *Where does she live with her small brood?* Surely they weren't one of the homeless families she had read about who lived under a bridge or in a cardboard box somewhere! Loraine felt her throat tighten and tears sting her eyes. *And here I am with an all-but-empty two-story house,* she thought guiltily. She wasn't ready to take in strangers yet, but. . .

"You do the turkey and dressing. I'll add the sauce and roll," a deep voice suggested beside her. The voice belonged to a man she'd never seen before who was wearing an apron like hers, smiling a wide smile that spilled over from dark brown eyes. She noted the turned-up corners of a generous mouth.

"I'm Ted," he added, taking the first plate from her, "new associate pastor at the church down the street."

"I'm Loraine," she answered, returning his smile gratefully as she struggled to regain the rhythm of her interrupted routine. *I don't care what weird denomination he represents,* she thought, recalling stories she had heard about that congregation, *so long as he helps serve this food!*

"God bless you, sir," she heard Ted say beside her as he handed the filled plate into the trembling hands of a red-faced man smelling of stale alcohol.

At least he will be drinking only tea or coffee with this meal, Loraine thought, pushing her hair back from her damp forehead with her right wrist and reaching for another plate with her left hand. Again, she glanced at the clock. She'd been serving for more than an hour, and the shuffling line still stretched halfway around the big room.

"There's no rest for the weary," Ted breathed beside her. She threw him a tired grimace and reached for another plate.

Finally, Ted was placing the last plate into the hands of an elderly man who let go of his grip on the counter to take it, then nearly dropped it as he clutched the counter again for support.

She saw Ted quickly come around the counter, take the plate in one hand and the elbow of the old man in the other. As he guided the man to the last empty place at one of the tables, Loraine leaned wearily against the wall behind her.

"Could you give us a hand with the cleanup?" Gloria asked hopefully.

Loraine thought longingly of her clean, quiet house, with Tigger asleep on the sofa and John Grisham waiting on the table. *I have the evening before me,* she reminded herself. *I have no all-night cooking, wrapping, or decorating to do. I am free to spend this time as I please, since I'm not really "doing" Christmas this year.* Looking into Gloria's tired, hopeful eyes, she knew she really couldn't refuse. She took a deep breath. "Sure," she agreed, glad to see that her answer brought some relief and a broad grin back to the woman's face.

Loraine removed the stainless steel pans from the heating elements on the counter and carried them to the big sinks in the back room. They had two automatic dishwashers back there, but the pans were done by hand. She placed one into the sink, turned on hot water, squirted soap into it, picked up a sponge, and began to scrub.

The two cooks, who had been there since 5:00 a.m.,

left, but Gloria was hard at work cleaning the stoves, and Peggy was in her office busy with paperwork. As Loraine went back and forth to gather soiled utensils, she could see Ted out in the dining room busily wiping tables, straightening chairs, and picking up trash.

When the cleanup was finished, Gloria handed her a filled plate. "Enjoy!" she ordered. "You've earned it."

"Thank you," she said, feeling her empty stomach rumble. It had been a long time since breakfast.

Gloria held a plate out to Ted, but he shook his head. "Thanks, but I've got to run," he said, taking off his apron and shrugging into the overcoat he had retrieved from one of the hooks in the hallway. "The men at church are delivering Angel Tree gifts later this evening," he explained to Loraine, "and I promised to coordinate our efforts. I enjoy that duty, though," he added. "It's such a joy to see little eyes light up at a special gift supposedly from a dad or a mom who is in prison. Most of them couldn't give their children anything for Christmas without the assistance of some program like Angel Tree, and many of them really do care."

She nodded. She had heard of the program on TV and among the many solicitations she received each week in the mail. Angel Tree was an outgrowth of Chuck Colson's Prison Fellowship, and she was sure it was a good cause. There were just so many appeals, and she couldn't help them all on retirement income—even though hers now seemed relatively comfortable after seeing the needy people here today. She threw loose change into the Salvation Army kettles each time she passed them, donated to the food pantry through her church, and sent small checks here and there for special needs.

"It's men only for the deliveries," Ted said, pulling on leather driving gloves, "but there is a get-together at the church afterward—a chance to fortify ourselves with some refreshment. You'd be more than welcome to join us," he offered.

Loraine shook her head. "I'm pretty well worn-out," she said with a smile, "and I have a good cat and a good book waiting for me at home."

"No family you need to prepare Christmas for?" he asked, his dark eyes searching hers. "No last-minute shopping, wrapping, cooking? My wife used to be up nearly all night sometimes these last two days before Christmas."

Again, she smiled and shook her head. "Been there and done that!" she replied. "But my son's in the Middle East this year, and my two daughters are—" She stopped, suddenly irritated at the man's prying. "They're away," she finished abruptly, removing her apron and tossing it in the bin for washing.

"No husband eagerly awaiting your return?" he probed.

"My husband is dead," she snapped, "and I'm spending Christmas alone for once. I plan to enjoy every quiet, peaceful moment of it!"

"I'm sorry," he said sincerely. "I didn't mean to pry. Maybe you can join us some other time." And giving her a wide, apologetic smile, he was gone.

A strange man, Loraine thought, digging into her turkey and dressing. *It depresses me to think of how many pitiful specimens of humanity have passed through this line today,* she thought. *Drug addicts, alcoholics, the homeless, the down-and-out, and the downright ornery, as Jack used to put it.*

She knew that Jack would have given the shirt off his back to someone who truly needed it, but he had little patience with those who wouldn't try to help themselves. This Ted had shown equal courtesy and kindness to even the most repulsive of their guests, sharing that wonderful smile with each of them, and walking away with his apparently natural cheerfulness intact.

A strange man, she repeated, taking her keys from her coat pocket and heading for the door.

Chapter 3

Back home Loraine took a hot shower followed by a short nap in the recliner between favorite segments of *Fox News*. Then she got out the popcorn popper, the jar of popcorn, and a bottle of vegetable oil. The lunch she had eaten down at the center was long gone, and it was time for a snack, she decided. One of her favorites was plain old-fashioned popcorn popped in hot oil and covered with salt. She didn't care what *anybody* said about it being bad for her cholesterol or her blood pressure or her triglycerides.

"If it tastes good, spit it out immediately!" her doctor had joked at her last visit, recommending a bland, low-fat diet. *Well, let young Dr. Spencer eat Styrofoam popcorn and soy burgers,* she thought defiantly. *I will eat what I please!*

Of course, as Dr. Spencer had reminded her, she didn't want to have a stroke or a heart attack and be an invalid, and generally she ate a fairly healthy diet. *But if I want a bowl of oil-popped popcorn covered in salt once in a while,* she thought, *I'll have it!*

She plugged in the popper and poured in oil and popcorn. Then she virtuously sliced a Granny Smith apple into a saucer and looked around for that John Grisham book, *Skipping Christmas.* She found it just in time to rescue the popcorn before it scorched.

Comfortably ensconced in the recliner, munching on popcorn and apple slices, she tried to settle down with her book again. As much as she enjoyed Grisham's writing, though, she couldn't focus on the story. Something was nagging at her—like the time she forgot to make Susan's potato salad, or the time she neglected to buy candy and trinkets for the stockings and had to send Jack out to buy what he could find at the last minute.

"It's just that it's the evening before Christmas Eve, and there's nothing that I have to do," she told herself smugly.

She got up and went through the house switching on lights. With the clocks back on standard time for the winter months, it was dark outside by six o'clock.

Usually, this was the day she and Jack had made an

evening of last-minute shopping and a quick dinner together amid the crowds. It was a ritual they had both looked forward to and insisted on keeping, even when they had to hire a babysitter because the children were not yet old enough to stay alone. Then she had stayed home on Christmas Eve to put the finishing touches on packages and food for that night's dinner and gift opening.

What is it like downtown tonight? she wondered, entertaining the thought of walking the three blocks to the shopping district to experience the small-town Christmas atmosphere without any personal urgency and watch the frantic crowds of shoppers without the stress of having anything to do to complete her own celebrations. *It would be a first!* she thought, the idea suddenly sounding appealing to her.

Loraine put on her coat and boots, wrapped a jaunty red scarf around her neck, and pulled on gloves to match. She was on the front stoop when it occurred to her that she should ask her next-door neighbor to accompany her. Esther surely had no last-minute Christmas duties to perform.

She glanced at the neat brick house next door. *Esther Cohen doesn't "do" Christmas,* she thought. *She keeps Hanukkah.* Each year, Loraine saw her lighting the eight-branched candelabra called a menorah on the table in her front window. She would add a candle each night until she reached the eighth one. This ritual commemorated the great miracle God had performed in keeping the temple menorah burning for eight days until more oil could be brought through enemy lines.

The year after Jack died, Esther, who had been a widow when she moved here, had invited Loraine over for latkes, delicious shredded potato pancakes eaten with sour cream and jellies. Then, while the menorah candles burned low, they had sung Hanukkah songs and played games with the little top Esther called a dreidel. They ate home-baked cookies in the shapes of menorahs, dreidels, and the six-sided Star of David, which Esther called the "Mogen David." Before Loraine had left, Esther had given her the recipe for latkes. Loraine still made them during Hanukkah when the holiday did not fall on the same busy days as Christmas.

She recalled the time she had asked at the Christian bookstore if they had Hanukkah cards, thinking she would send one to Esther. The horrified clerk had responded, "Certainly not!" She supposed she should have enlightened him that the Jewish holiday was simply the commemoration of a great miracle God had performed. It was no more anti-Christian than the parting of the Red Sea, the manna in the desert, or the providing of oil and flour for the widow in Elijah's time.

"O Hanukkah, O Hanukkah! Come light the menorah!" She sang softly the happy little song Esther had taught her and that she had passed on to her own children. What were the next lines? "*Dum de dum dum dum, de, dum, dum dum dum dum,*" she hummed as she went back inside and pulled off her gloves. "There'll be dreidels to play with and latkes to eat," she remembered. Then came her favorite part of the song, where the tempo slowed and the words became nostalgic: "And while we are playing, the candles are burning low. One for each night, they shed a sweet light to remind us of days long ago," she sang.

She might not have all the words right. Her children had often teased her about making up her own words to songs she couldn't remember, and sometimes even her own tune. But it was a nice little song for a beautiful holiday. "The Festival of Lights" Esther called it.

And Esther is a beautiful lady, Loraine thought warmly. They weren't "bosom buddies," just friendly neighbors who had shared many things over the years. She enjoyed having her as a next-door neighbor, the kind with whom she could exchange cookies and new recipes, who would lend her a cup of sugar if she ran out in the midst of her usual frantic baking splurge before Christmas or give her a ride to the supermarket if her car was in the shop.

Loraine turned and looked out the window to her right. The Mitchells' house next door was temporarily empty because they had gone to visit their daughter and new grandson in Colorado for the holidays. Beyond that, twenty years ago, Mr. Feroz and his quiet little wife had built a small stone house to resemble the houses of their native Iraq. The son they raised there had now grown up and moved away.

Esther was convinced that the Feroz's son had gone back to the Middle East to become a suicide bomber. She spat on the ground whenever Loraine mentioned the family. Although there was no reason to believe that the Feroz boy had done any such thing, she knew that Esther's anger arose from the loss of an uncle and his family killed in a suicide bombing in Tel Aviv.

Mrs. Feroz had died last year of cancer. Loraine could almost see her now, creeping out of the house behind her husband, only her beautiful dark eyes visible above the scarf tucked securely around her hair and face. She had never seen the woman's face, never known her first name. On those rare occasions when she met up with her, Loraine had simply addressed her as Mrs. Feroz.

Mr. Feroz, of course, did not keep Christmas, either. He kept Ramadan, fasting all day and feasting all night, or at least that was what she had heard. His Islamic beliefs were not something Loraine could share. His Allah was not the same God she and Esther worshiped. However, as an American, she respected his right to believe as he chose, and they exchanged friendly conversation when they met on evening walks or when she shopped at his little market a couple of blocks away.

As far as she could tell, Mr. Feroz had no family or friends here. Like Esther, he attended worship services in a larger nearby town.

Loraine laid down her gloves and picked up the phone. "Esther!" she said when her friend answered. "Would you be interested in a walk downtown to watch the crowds tonight, and perhaps a little something at the tea shop?"

"Loraine? Aren't you frantically into your Christmas preparations? Oh, I'm sorry," she said. "I forgot that this year you are as alone as I am." She hesitated then said, "Of course. I'd love to go with you, so long as you don't expect me to celebrate the birth of Yeshua. You know I don't believe—"

"I know, Esther. I may disagree with you on Jesus being the Messiah, but I promise not to bring that up tonight. I'm sure we'll see more of Santa Claus than Jesus, anyway. Come and go with me. It will be fun!"

"All right. Just let me put on my coat and boots. I'll meet you out front in five minutes," she promised.

Esther always makes my five-foot-three seem tall, Loraine thought as her diminutive neighbor joined her on the sidewalk, merry brown eyes peering out from the fur-lined hood of a warm parka.

"Oiy, what a night!" Esther exclaimed as they set off briskly toward the center of town, their breath forming frosty, cartoonlike blurbs on the air in front of them. "We could surely reach out and touch that evening star!"

Loraine looked up. "I believe we could, Esther," she agreed, wondering if it had looked that way on the night the angels appeared to the shepherds to announce the good news of the Savior's birth. Still, she was sure the supernova hanging over the manger in Bethlehem that night had been bigger than this ordinary evening star.

She took a deep breath, feeling the invigorating sting of the crisp, cold air in her nostrils then traveling down into her lungs. She noted the fuzzy glow of street-lights outlined against the nearly black velvet sky, and all around them the decorations of the season—gaily blinking multicolored lights, Santa scenes on the rooftops and lawns. Here and there a lighted crèche depicted the birth of Jesus, or Yeshua, as Esther called him.

Loraine wanted to say, "This really is what Christmas is all about, Esther, 'that white-hot moment when eternity melted into time,' as her pastor had described it. It was the moment when God sent his Son to become Emmanuel, God with us." But she had promised Esther not to talk about such things.

In minutes they were at the edge of the shopping district. They slowed their steps, enjoying the brightly lit shop windows, the gaiety of Christmas tunes blaring from loudspeakers, the spicy scent of evergreen, and the festive air of small-town Christmas.

In front of Hale's Department Store, Loraine saw the familiar red kettle of the Salvation Army hanging from its tripod. She dug in her pockets for something to contribute, but Esther turned away and peered into the shop window where a miniature train wailed through a Christmas village.

I suppose she has her own charities and doesn't want to contribute to anything having to do with the scorned Yeshua,

Loraine thought, pulling out a crumpled dollar bill and reaching out to drop it into the kettle.

Suddenly, she recognized the figure standing beside the kettle. Wearing a red and white Santa hat and vigorously ringing his bell was the pastor she had met earlier at the soup kitchen.

"Thank you," he said with that infectious grin. "Merry Christmas!"

She grinned back. "Merry Christmas, yourself," she answered. "But what are you doing here? I thought you were out delivering Angel Tree gifts."

"It's our church's day to help the Army with its annual drive," he explained. "It's my first year, but I understand they have done it for several years now. We're doing Angel Tree later. The gifts all are wrapped, tagged, and ready, but, you know, Santa always comes after the children are 'snug in their beds.'"

"Of course," she said. "Well, you look very chic in your fur hat," she added, trying unsuccessfully to picture her own pastor in the ridiculous getup.

"Thank you," he said primly, his eyes twinkling as a full-fledged grin took over.

Loraine became aware of Esther's questioning glance. "I've got to go," she whispered. "I'm giving my Jewish neighbor a small taste of our Christian Christmas."

"Really?" His eyebrows rose. "I'm surprised that she's willing. I mean, I'm aware that our Christian faith is built on a firm foundation of Judaism, but doesn't she believe the Messiah is yet to come?"

"Yes," Loraine answered, "but other than that, our beliefs are almost exactly the same. And I enjoy her company," she added.

"Oh, there's nothing wrong with being friends," he agreed. Then a frown wrinkled his forehead. "But if a person is wrong about Jesus Christ, it doesn't really matter what else he is right about," he said. "Your friend needs to know the Savior, Loraine." Coins rattled into the kettle, and he turned to acknowledge the contribution with a "Thank you. Merry Christmas!"

Loraine sensed that he turned back immediately to say something else to her, but she had already moved over to join Esther at the shop window.

"I give to Coats for Kids and Feed the Children," Esther explained defensively.

"Good for you," Loraine answered. "Let's go inside out of the cold."

They let the crowd carry them through a swinging shop door into the milling throng snatching last-minute bargains from the scrambled mess on the counters inside. Loraine took in the ropes of holly, ivy, and pine, with their red velvet bows and brightly colored ornaments, suspended from the walls and ceiling and twined around every post. *I guess I really have missed my decorations this year,* she admitted to herself, *though I haven't missed all this frantic hullabaloo.*

Above the din of voices, a fat man in a red and white suit sitting on a throne at the center of the store boomed, "Ho! Ho! Ho! Merry Christmas! Merry Christmas!" A throng of children waited to climb onto his knee and whisper their requests, while parents and grandparents strained to hear so they could ensure the granting of those requests.

Gradually, Loraine became aware of the scowling expressions of irritated shoppers and the sheer exhaustion in the faces of harassed clerks. She winced at the jab of a heedless elbow and the crunch of a heavy shoe on her left foot. When she was assaulted by a spate of vulgar language from the lips of a pretty young girl standing beside them, she threw an apologetic glance at Esther, who was hunched defensively against a post studying a poster advertising a brand of alcohol as the perfect "spirit of Christmas."

"See, Esther," she pointed out, "the modern Christmas is mostly Santa Claus, presents, food, and alcohol."

Esther gave her a wry grin. "They don't carry Hanukkah cards, either," she said sympathetically.

Loraine grinned back. "Let's get out of here and go to the tea shop," she suggested.

"Whew!" Esther breathed, removing her furry hood and then her coat when they finally were seated at a small round table in the back. "I think I'm glad I only have to buy a few presents and make some latkes and cookies for Hanukkah. I'd never make it through one of your Christmases!"

"I think you're right!" Loraine sighed, massaging the boot over her injured foot. "I've forgotten how bad it can be out there! Jack and I used to enjoy this last night of shopping, but now I wonder why. It must have been just the fact that it was time we always spent together."

Esther nodded. "It's been nearly twenty years, and I still miss Jacob." She pronounced it "Ya-a-cov." "Zal," she added. Then seeing Loraine's puzzled look, she translated, "May he rest in peace."

Loraine patted the older woman's hand, then took the menu a waitress extended. "I think I'll have spiced tea and a couple of those wonderful raisin cookies they make here," she said. "What's for you, Esther?"

Esther ran her gaze over the small menu. "I'll have

the carrot cake and plain tea," she decided, handing back the menu.

As they waited for their orders, Loraine said, "I'm sorry, Esther. I guess this nostalgic visit downtown at the peak of the Christmas frenzy wasn't such a good idea after all."

Esther nodded in agreement, then smiled. "I guess you needed to get it out of your system," she said. "I don't regret trying it once. We just won't do it again soon!"

When their food came, Esther was telling a story about one of her children wanting to become a Christian one year just so she could share in her friends' Christmas. "She wanted to be Jewish for Hanukkah and just convert to Christianity for the Christmas season!" she explained.

Loraine laughed, breaking off a piece of cookie to dip into her tea. Then she said seriously, "Maybe your daughter had the right idea, Esther. We have so much in common. It's a shame we can't just share the best of our beliefs and not squabble over the differences."

She remembered Ted's comment earlier, "If a person is wrong about Jesus Christ, it doesn't really matter what else he is right about." She knew that in the eternal scheme of things that was true, but she had told Esther what she believed. She couldn't force her to accept it.

Esther looked up from her cake. "Our own little 'road map to peace'?" she said with a grin. "Now, if we can just get America and all the countries of the Middle East to accept it—shalom!"

They were laughing as they left the shop and made their way home, going a couple of blocks out of their way to avoid the downtown mob.

When Loraine left Esther at her front door, she automatically called out, "Merry Christmas!"

"Laylah tov! Good night!" Esther responded with a twinkle in her eye. Then she added, "Happy Hanukkah!"

Laughing, Loraine let herself into her house. She undressed and put on her gown and robe. Finally, slipping her tired feet into soft, warm slippers, she picked up John Grisham's book.

"I've put the ghost of December twenty-third to rest," she told Tigger, satisfied that she truly had. The big cat looked at her as though he understood and came over to nestle beside her in the recliner where she could scratch his ears while she read more about skipping Christmas.

Chapter 4

Loraine was up and dressed by seven, as had become her custom as she had grown older. She might take a small nap in the recliner in the afternoon, but she generally could not lie in bed after seven in the morning.

She filled Tigger's water bowl and warmed him a small bowl of milk in the microwave. It was a habit she had developed while caring for the small, orphaned kitten. Tigger had been the last of a litter of kittens being given away in the Wal-Mart parking lot. She couldn't bear to think of that small, striped ball of fur with the frightened yellow eyes being taken off to the pound. Immediately he had claimed her for his own. *That's what Tiggers do best!* she remembered thinking.

While the house was so full of Jack and the children

and their possessions, Tigger lived on the back porch. But now that she was alone, Loraine let him share the big empty house, grateful for his companionship. "And you expect warm milk in your bowl every morning, don't you, old buddy?" she said, reaching down to pat him on his broad, striped head. He purred an "uh huh" and went right on lapping up warm milk.

Loraine filled the teakettle with cold water, set it on the burner, and turned on the stove. Then she took her favorite Christmas mug down from the cupboard and dropped a teabag into it. Next, she sliced a piece of date bread, placed it on a small paper plate, and carried it to the table. It wasn't that she particularly wanted date bread, though she did like it. She was just determined not to cook today.

As she ate and sipped her tea, she read about the Savior's birth in the second chapter of Luke. Closing her eyes, she remembered back to Christmas Eves past— once the family was finished with dinner and before any gifts were opened, they always took turns reading that chapter.

She could almost hear Beth lisping through missing teeth, "And there were in that thame country, shepheths abiding in the field. . . ." She could picture Susan sitting primly in her small rocking chair awaiting her turn and little Jack, still too young to read, squirming impatiently on the hearth. He was always eager to get to the presents they would be allowed to open before going to bed. Contributions left by "Santa" in the night—those mysterious packages that appeared on the hearth and the stuffed stockings hanging from the mantel—were dealt with on Christmas morning.

After throwing her empty plate in the trash and rinsing the tea mug at the sink, Lorainc looked around for something to do. The bird feeders looked nearly full from the kitchen window, but she put on her coat and boots and went out to replenish them anyway.

A fresh snow had fallen during the night. *It's a beautiful Christmas Eve day,* Loraine thought, *clear and crisp, with the sun's rays picking out diamonds in the grass and along the tree limbs, and the bright red cardinals completing the picture. Beth would be out here with her camera. Little Jack would be begging to go sledding. Susan would be wanting to make snow cream, and Jack would be shaking his head, saying he couldn't understand how they could fool their stomachs that way.* She smiled at the fond memories and felt a wave of longing wash over her.

She was confident that she knew where Jack was, but what was he doing up there in heaven this very moment? Could he see her down here feeding the birds, spending Christmas alone for the first time in all these years? After all the laments he had heard her make about not having enough time, was he laughing at her efforts to find ways to fill the hours this year?

What were her children doing? Was little Jack sweltering in the Middle Eastern sun? Was he in some kind of danger? She said a quick prayer for his protection, then realized that it likely was evening over there, with the hot sun sinking into the desert. Perhaps he and his buddies were playing cards or resting for the night. Susan was probably visiting with yet another group of new in-laws, and Beth surely was out somewhere exploring Italy with her ever-present camera. In her last telephone call, she had mentioned someone named Roberto, more than once.

Anyway, Loraine felt sure that none of her family members were alone this Christmas. *I'm the only one alone this year, rattling around this big old house, trying to find something to occupy my time,* she thought. *But I'm not having a pity party here,* she reminded herself. *I'm enjoying the peace of a stress-free holiday for the first time in thirty-five years!*

Her thoughts went to Esther Cohen next door. Last night Esther had asked her not to talk about her belief that the Old Testament's promised Messiah had come. Loraine knew that Pastor Ted was right. Esther, like everybody else, needed the Savior. They had discussed this before, more than once, and Loraine knew that no matter how convinced she was that her beliefs were right, she could not force them on her friend. They had enjoyed a pleasant evening together in spite of that one major difference in their beliefs and the mayhem they had encountered downtown.

She could not see the front of Esther's house from here, but she knew there were no Christmas lights outlining its eaves and windows. In contrast, the Mitchells' house on the other side of hers was lit by a string of Christmas lights that they had programmed to come on with the house lights to convince would-be robbers they were not out in Colorado visiting their children for the holidays.

Beyond that, the Feroz place would be dark. Mr. Feroz certainly did not decorate for the Christian holiday. How did he handle this time that so absorbed most of his neighbors, those his Qur'an called "infidels"? Did he just retreat inside his house until the commotion was over, going out only to run his shop or to visit his place of worship in the next town?

The question Loraine had to deal with, however, was not what Mr. Feroz or Esther Cohen did while the whole town, the nation, most of the world was caught up in celebrating some version of the birth of Jesus Christ. The question was what she was going to do today to pass the time until the midnight service at church tonight. *It's unbelievable that I have absolutely nothing to do on Christmas Eve!* she marveled.

Loraine sat down at her desk in the family room and pulled out some notepaper. She wrote notes to some out-of-town friends and one to her Aunt Caroline in Georgia, addressed the envelopes, stamped them, and laid them by her purse to mail the next time she was out.

Now what? she thought. *Should I make some more date bread?* No, she decided. In addition to the one she had cut, there was another fresh loaf wrapped in foil in the cupboard. It wasn't likely she would finish both of them before they molded. Should she prepare something for her own quiet dinner tonight or for lunch tomorrow? She had baked a small country ham and made a fruit salad two days ago that she hadn't touched yet.

She threw a small load of laundry into the washer, added detergent, and turned it on. She ran the dust mop over the polished hardwood floors and a wet mop over the linoleum in the kitchen area. She wiped off the counter and the stove-top. She watered the vines in the window over the sink. Then she wandered through the house straightening pictures and lamp shades that were already straight.

At noon, Loraine fixed a ham sandwich and ate it with a small helping of fruit salad and a glass of iced tea. Then she puttered around the house rearranging the figures in both nativity scenes, making a new street of shops and houses in the Dickens village, which she kept year-round on the top shelves of her grandmother's poplar cupboard in the living room.

She glanced at the bare mantel, debating whether or not to hang stockings from it just for old-times' sake. *That would be foolish*, she decided at last. It could only serve as a painful reminder that her loved ones weren't here to take them down and exclaim excitedly over the contents that always had appeared in them "magically" during the night, even in the years long after Santa was expected. She remembered fondly that it had been her last chore—putting candies and small treasures into the stockings before falling into bed for a couple of hours of exhausted sleep before the early risers were up.

It was nearly dark now, she noted, flipping on the light. Only a few more hours and it would be time to get dressed for the midnight service. She went to the closet and rummaged through it, trying to decide what to wear. *Something appropriately red or green*, she thought, shoving the hangers and their contents back and forth on the rod. Maybe she would wear the red velvet pantsuit since she wore it only during the Christmas season.

Suddenly, she heard carolers out front begin a joyful, if not so melodious, rendition of "It Came upon a Midnight Clear." *I'm not going to invite them in for hot chocolate!* she promised herself, stifling a twinge of guilt as she peered out from behind the living room draperies.

The streetlight at the corner revealed that they were not from her church, but from various congregations around town. She recognized Bessie Adams, Maude Simpson, and Bill Thomas. And there were Sam Curtis and Alma Tate. There were a few faces she did not recognize scattered through the impromptu choir. *Must be a group of volunteers from the Senior Citizens' Center,* she decided, noting that all of them appeared to be her age or older.

I've always wanted to go caroling, she thought wistfully, *but there just never was enough time.*

"Time is something I have plenty of this year," she reminded herself.

Smiling, she put on her boots and her coat, pulled the front door shut behind her, and dropped the key into her pocket.

Chapter 5

"W elcome!" Sam Curtis called as Loraine came down the sidewalk toward the group. "Come share my songbook!"

Loraine wondered if she had made a mistake in joining the group. Sam was a widower who had retired from his hardware business a couple of years ago. She had known him all her life, had gone to grade school with him. She knew that he and his wife had raised six children, who, with their families, were scattered all over the country. His wife had died suddenly last year of a heart attack. Not wanting to hurt his feelings, she accepted half of his offered songbook and began to fit her husky alto into the so-called harmony of the carolers.

Having thoroughly serenaded Loraine's street, the group moved on to another block. There had been no sign of Esther or Mr. Feroz, but she had not expected them to appear. The Christian carols probably did little more than irritate them.

She thought their singing was getting better, but maybe it was just her imagination, an illusion created by being part of the singers rather than a captive listener. She hoped they were a blessing to those who heard them and not an irritant.

Sam smiled at her warmly, showing yellowed teeth with a gap where he had lost a couple right in the front bottom half of his mouth. *Is he too tight to get a bridge put in?* she wondered, recalling stories she had heard over the years of his stinginess with his wife and children. *Or maybe he's just wrapped up in a deluded notion of his own attractiveness.* Loraine remembered that he had been that way even as a child. *Maybe he doesn't think we'll notice,* she thought, smiling at the few long, gray hairs combed across his extensive bald spot.

Sam hooked his left arm through her right elbow and gave her a suggestive leer from under slightly raised eyebrows. Loraine shuddered involuntarily and carefully removed her arm from his grasp. As casually as possible, she eased over to stand between Sophia Carter and Ilene Tussey, hardly missing a word of "—and loud and deep, their words repeat of peace on

Earth, goodwill to men."

A little later, she threw a sideways glance at Sam and saw that he was sharing his book with Alma Tate, who seemed delighted by the attention. Loraine sighed in relief and entered wholeheartedly into the singing in front of the apartments for the elderly and then the Senior Citizens' Center, where lonely people had gathered for a pleasant evening of board games and cookies and punch.

Suddenly, Loraine heard a new, deep baritone voice bolster the weak contributions of the men around her. She looked around to see Ted, the new associate pastor she had met in the food line at the soup kitchen and downtown ringing his bell for the Salvation Army. He was standing in the back row singing with gusto, though slightly off-key. He gave her a warm smile that lit up his dark eyes. So what if Ted was a pastor and married. She had no designs on him, and she was sure he had none on her, except as a potential convert for his church, perhaps. She returned the smile.

As they trudged along the street to the next residential neighborhood, Loraine found Ted beside her.

"Did you get the Angel Tree gifts delivered last night?" she asked.

"We did!" he affirmed, blowing absently on cold and

reddened hands. "Those children were so excited! Three of them were in the food line yesterday with their mother. She was so overwhelmed by her kids getting gifts that she cried. It was a very gratifying experience." He ended quickly as the group took up its next song.

All at once, Loraine noticed that he was wearing only a thin jacket and his hands were gloveless. If she remembered correctly, Ted had worn an overcoat and gloves when he left the soup kitchen yesterday afternoon. Last night, too, he had worn them, along with his furry Santa Claus hat, as he rang his bell over the Salvation Army kettle. She couldn't remember if he had worn a hat before, but his head was bare now, the streetlight overhead picking up silver highlights in his thick, dark hair.

She glanced around. All the other men wore overcoats and gloves, and most of them had on sock caps or hats of some kind. "Where are your overcoat and gloves?" she whispered between verses of "O Little Town of Bethlehem." She was surprised to see a flush creep over his face as he stuffed his hands into the pockets of his inadequate jacket.

The woman standing on the other side of the pastor leaned toward Loraine. "He probably gave them to some homeless man on the street," she whispered. "We can't keep warm clothes on the man. He's always giving them away!"

"Now, Shirley!" Ted admonished. "Anyway, he was wearing some thin old cast-off suit coat and shivering. I've got more clothes at home. I just didn't have time to go get them."

"Yeah, right!" the woman answered sarcastically. "Pastor Hammons, I just don't know what we're going to do with you!" But Loraine noticed that she smiled up at him fondly and patted him on the arm.

Loraine thought of her own pastor, so dignified in his tailored suits and designer ties. She respected the man. He was an excellent speaker and had been faithful to visit, or to send someone else to visit, two or three times a week during Jack's illness. But lately she had become a little disenchanted with his politically correct sermons. When she asked him to have the congregation participate in the day of prayer for Israel this past October, he had nodded agreeably but done nothing. The day had passed without notice so far as her congregation was concerned.

She had grown very interested in the plight of Israelis because of Esther. Born in Tel Aviv, Esther had relatives and friends there still. After every bombing, Loraine grieved with her friend for those killed, for the orphans left behind, for parents deprived of their children, for the maimed who could no longer earn a living or take care of themselves.

Whenever she could, Loraine sent small contributions to help the survivors of this never ending struggle with those who were determined to drive the Jews from their tiny piece of land.

Her thoughts went back to the Old Testament story of Abraham and his two sons, Ishmael and Isaac. *How sad,* she thought, *that Abraham's giving in to his childless wife's pleading to have a son by her handmaid has resulted in centuries of bitter hatred between the descendants of two half brothers.*

Loraine felt that she could understand Ishmael's resentment at being cast out into the desert by his father as a result of the strife between his mother, the gloating handmaid, and her vengeful mistress, Sarah. She could understand how that resentment had been passed down for generations. And she could understand why the descendants of Sarah's son, Isaac, clung so desperately to the little country called Israel that they had carved out of a small portion of the land given to them by God through Abraham so long ago.

What a mess we make of things, she thought, *when we try to "help" God fulfill His promises!* She had thought the least her church could do was join in the international prayers for the "peace of Jerusalem" planned for that one day.

Only twice in the seven years that he has been my pastor have I asked him to do something special, she thought with a twinge of resentment, *and both times he either forgot or decided to ignore my request. Perhaps it's time I found another place of worship.* Loraine couldn't help but feel envious as she watched the warmth and camaraderie between Ted and Shirley.

Instantly, she was contrite and asked God to forgive her for envy and harboring a grudge against her pastor. What was it the angel had said to the shepherds? "On earth, peace to men of goodwill," she believed one version put it. Where was her goodwill?

"Come on, slowpoke," Ted joked, reaching out one bare hand to pull her from her disturbing thoughts back into the group. They were heading up a walk to the front door of the house they had just serenaded. "The Nelsons have invited us in for coffee and hot chocolate."

Loraine hesitated, then took his cold hand and let him lead her past a life-sized Santa and sleigh pulled by all eight reindeer and Rudolph—complete with a blinking red nose. The front door was outlined by multicolored lights and decorated with a huge wreath of real candy canes.

"Coffee or chocolate?" Ted asked when they were inside. Lights and ornaments dangled from a vaulted ceiling, and a twelve-foot pine tree glowed regally in one corner.

"Oh, I've always felt that sleigh riding and caroling call for hot chocolate," she said. She took the mug he handed her from the table in the center of the room and stirred the miniature marshmallows with a plastic spoon. Gingerly sipping the hot liquid, she walked around exploring the whimsical displays on every available surface. She couldn't help but think of her own decorations still packed away in boxes in the attic. *But I won't be up all night New Year's Eve packing them away again,* she thought smugly.

"You're grinning like the proverbial cat that swallowed the canary," Ted said, coming up beside her. He held a cup of coffee in one hand and a large brownie in the other. "What's so satisfying?"

"I was just thinking of my uncluttered Christmas this year," she answered. Then, suddenly wanting to be at home enjoying it, she added, "I need to get home."

"I'll walk you back," he offered instantly. "Where do you live?" When she told him, he said, "We're about four blocks from there. Are you too tired to walk?"

She shook her head. "No, I'm fine, and you don't need to—"

"It's dark out there, and walking home alone is not a good idea," he said firmly. "Criminals take advantage of times like this when people are so absorbed in their celebrations."

"But it's cold out there, and you don't even have an overcoat!" she protested.

"I've got to go that way, or part of it, anyway. Come on," he said, "time's a wastin'!"

Loraine let him take her by the elbow and steer her outside, both of them murmuring thanks to their host and hostess and saying good night to their fellow carolers on the way.

As they walked through the frosty night, Loraine found herself laughing at Ted's comical stories of his own childhood Christmases and those when his two children, both grown now, had been at home.

"Those were good days," he sighed. "Hectic, but good."

She nodded, recalling those boisterous Christmases when Jack and all three children were home. She could almost see the lights on the tree, smell the turkey and dressing baking in the oven, hear the happy voices raised in excitement. "Yes, I know what you mean," she agreed. "I was exhausted by the time Christmas Day got here, but those were good days."

"I miss Regina and the boys," he said then, "sometimes so badly I can hardly stand it. But I know Randy and Craig are busy with their own lives now, and Regina is in a much better place."

"Your wife is—" she began in surprise.

"—in heaven," he finished with surety. "If anybody's there, Regina is."

"I'm sorry," Loraine blurted. She had assumed that he had a wife. Hadn't he said she stayed up all night getting ready for Christmas like she had for so many years? "I mean, I'm not sorry she's in heaven," she stammered. "I'm just—"

"I know," he rushed to her rescue, "you're sorry for my loss. So am I, but how was it Edna St. Vincent Millay put it? 'Life must go on, though good men die,'" he quoted. "'Life must go on; I forget just why.'"

"My husband was a good man who loved the Lord with all his heart, though he had his own way of showing it," she broke in. "But he was a pillar of our church, a good role model for the children, a strong arm for me to lean on. He never met a stranger, and he never hesitated to say exactly what he thought. He had a sarcastic sense of humor that sometimes made me laugh, sometimes embarrassed me, and sometimes irritated me. I miss him terribly at times," she added softly.

He nodded. "Yes, I know what you mean, but life does go on, and it doesn't do any good to sit around moping over what we've lost. At least we've had something really special and good, something some people never experience." He smiled that contagious smile. "Your husband and my wife are up there somewhere together tonight, and here we are."

She smiled up at him, then looked away, suddenly uncomfortable. "Here's my house," she said, fumbling in her coat pocket for the key.

His hand on her arm stopped her flight. "It's been a nice evening, Loraine," he said seriously, looking her straight in the eyes. "You don't mind if I call you Loraine, do you?"

She shook her head. "Of course not." She grasped the key and held it up, feeling relieved without quite knowing why. "Well, it's been a long day, and I can't wait to sit down with a good book and relax. Good night," she added.

"Merry Christmas," he answered, his eyes studying hers for a moment. Then he turned and walked away, back in the direction from which they had come.

Loraine went into the house and quickly locked the

door behind her, as though something threatening might be lurking outside. She took a deep, steadying breath and bent to remove her boots. Her feet were nearly frozen, she realized, but she had a warm feeling inside.

My first caroling venture was a totally satisfying experience even if I did have to fend off the attentions of Sam Curtis, she thought, removing her coat and scarf. She was even less interested in some lonely old widower with missing teeth and hair combed carefully over his bald spot than she was in a traditional Christmas celebration.

The warm brown eyes and wide, friendly smile of the associate pastor came into her thoughts, but she pushed them away. *He's just interested in a new convert for his church, and I have no interest in any man.*

"It's you and me against the world, Tigger, and I like it that way," she vowed, stroking the cat, who purred his agreement.

She ate a bowl of fruit salad, smiling over the efforts of John Grisham's hero to skip Christmas by taking his wife on a cruise. *I've been more successful than he has,* she thought smugly. To be honest, though, she had done more Christmassy things than she ever had intended. *But after the candlelight service tonight,* she promised herself, *I'm going to do absolutely nothing until December twenty-sixth, if then.*

She read awhile longer, then took a shower and dressed in the red velvet pantsuit. At exactly 10:30 p.m., she was backing the car out of the driveway on her way to the church.

This ancient English-style church is beautiful any time, Loraine thought as she walked through the tall, double doors into the sanctuary, *but it always looks its best at Christmas with candles burning under hurricane lamps nestled in holly on the wide stone windowsills and greenery entwining its posts and altar rails.*

Taking a small white candle in its paper skirt from the usher, she chose a pew about halfway down the middle aisle. She sat there enjoying the ambiance of history and tradition until the robed choir members and pastors came down the aisle, two by two, carrying lighted candles and singing "Ring Out, Wild Bells!" Rising with the congregation to join in the last verse, she gasped as Ted Hammons appeared beside her.

"What are you doing here?" she whispered, moving over to make room on the pew.

"We don't have a midnight service, so I decided to join yours," he whispered back, taking the left side of her hymnal and adding his off-key baritone to the chorus.

Loraine was a little aggravated by his presence. She had looked forward to this quiet time of worship just between herself and God, but she guessed it would be selfish to deny someone else the same blessing. *This is my favorite service of the entire year, and nobody is going to destroy my delight in it,* she told herself firmly.

Loraine couldn't help being conscious of Ted there beside her, though, as they sang the familiar carols, listened to the minister's perfectly planned and executed message, and walked down the aisle to the altar to take part in communion. Back in the pew, she joined in singing "Silent Night," while Ted dipped his candlewick into the flame of the usher's candle. Then, lighting her candle from his, she held it high overhead as the service ended with the usual rousing "Joy to the World!"

I'm not going anywhere for coffee or tea or anything, so don't ask! she told him silently as he waited for the crowd to thin so they could ease into the aisle.

He moved ahead of her to the front entry, dropped his candle into the box on the table, and shook the minister's hand. Outside on the steps, he turned to her. "Well, it's officially here," he said. "Merry Christmas!"

"Merry Christmas," she answered. She watched as he disappeared into the crowd, leaving her only the memory of his grin. *No, thank you, I didn't want to go for coffee,* she thought, *but I might have liked to be asked so I could refuse!*

Laughing at her childish response, she headed home, exulting in a Christmas Eve with no last-minute presents to wrap, no stockings to fill, no food to prepare. It was an unheard of phenomenon, one she looked forward to with great pleasure, she told herself firmly.

Chapter 6

It's raining! Loraine thought, stretching luxuriously under the covers. *There's nothing I like better than rain on the roof while I sleep. It will wash away our Christmas snow, but at least we had it for Christmas Eve.*

She glanced at the clock. "Seven-thirty!" she gasped. "On Christmas Day? It's time to get up!" She threw off the covers and searched for her slippers with bare feet reluctant to touch the cold floor. Then, slowly, she sank back onto the edge of the bed. It was Christmas Day, all right, but she had absolutely nothing to do.

"Incredible!" she breathed. Back when the kids were home, there would have been paper knee deep in the living room and cast-off ribbon tangling around her ankles as she tried to escape to the kitchen to put Jack's scalloped oysters in the oven and to start their traditional sausage and scrambled eggs. And if, like this year, the day didn't fall on a Sunday, the children would have spent the rest of the day divesting the stockings of their treasures, eating leftovers, and sitting around fingering their new possessions with glazed, satiated expressions on their faces.

In those days, she wouldn't have imagined being alone on Christmas Day. She sighed, feeling a little hollow inside as she slipped on a pair of faded jeans and a blue sweatshirt sporting a scene of evergreens in the snow. She added socks and loafers before going to the bathroom mirror to run a comb through her hair.

The green-eyed image of an aging woman stared back at her. She studied it for a moment, then stuck out her tongue. "You can get old if you want to," she told the reflection, "but I'm going to go right on enjoying life as long as I have it! So there!" *And I'm going to enjoy this peaceful Christmas Day if it's the last thing I do!* she vowed.

Loraine sliced off a piece of the date bread and turned on the teakettle, looking out the window, where a few small birds braved the rain to feast at the half-empty bird feeders. There was no need to venture out into the wet to refill them yet.

She went to the refrigerator to get Tigger's milk, but when she picked up the jug, she could tell it was nearly empty. She removed the cap and turned the jug upside down, but only a trickle of milk ran out into the bowl. She warmed it in the microwave, anyway, and set it down for the cat.

Tigger lapped up the meager offering and looked up at her reproachfully. *"Meow?"* he questioned.

"I'm sorry, old buddy, that's all I've got. I'll have to go to the—" She stopped. Even the supermarket, which stayed open day and night, would be closed today. Why hadn't she thought to replenish the milk yesterday while she was out running around doing everything else?

Then she thought of Mr. Feroz's market a couple of streets over. Surely he wouldn't be closed for the Christian holiday!

"I'll get you some milk in a little while, Tigger," she promised, opening a small can of tuna and spooning it into his bowl to compensate. The cat sniffed at it disdainfully, sampled a bite or two, then jumped up onto the couch. He turned his back and began taking an elaborate spit bath, giving her an unmistakable cold shoulder.

Loraine laughed and sat down at the table with her date bread and tea. She picked up her much worn NIV

Bible, and it fell open to her favorite book, Isaiah. Chapter 58. Her eyes fell on verse 10. "If you spend yourselves in behalf of the hungry and satisfy the needs of the oppressed, then your light will rise in the darkness, and your night will become like the noonday." *Should I take these words as a commendation for my work at the soup kitchen the other day or an admonishment to do something more today?* she wondered.

She got up, threw away her empty paper plate, and rinsed out her cup. "Might as well get that trip to the market over with," she said aloud, going to the hall closet for her coat, scarf, and boots.

As she passed the phone, she hesitated. *Should I call Esther to see if she needs anything?* she wondered. Then she remembered Esther's feelings for Mr. Feroz. She absolutely refused to have anything to do with him—that included using anything from his market.

Loraine grabbed her purse and keys and headed for the garage. She got into the car, started it, and gave it a few moments to warm up. *If that were snow drifting down out there instead of heavy rain, I'd have walked,* she thought, putting the car into gear and backing slowly out onto the pavement. Actually, she liked walking in the rain, too, but not in a soaking downpour on a cold day.

She maneuvered the car onto the street and drove

carefully to the market, where she was surprised to find a parking place right out front. Then she remembered that it was Christmas Day. Everyone was shut inside four warm, safe walls with their loved ones. A wave of longing swept over her.

"Nonsense!" she scolded. "My living room is straight, my dishes are clean, and I have had seven or eight hours of sleep." Beth and Susan both had called the night before, and maybe even little Jack would be able to get a line out sometime today or tomorrow. "What more could I want?" she asked, chuckling as she parked and headed into the market.

The small dark man behind the cash register looked up as the bell over the door announced her presence. "Good morning, dear lady," he greeted her in his usual way, but his lips did not bear his customary smile, and his eyes seemed troubled.

"What's wrong, Mr. Feroz?" she asked, without thinking that he might find the question an intrusion into his privacy.

He sighed, then gave that typical Middle Eastern shrug. "Ah, nothing to worry your head about, dear lady," he replied in perfect English, but with a thick accent that had not lessened during his many years in America. "The question is, what are you doing here on your busy holiday? Ah, I suspect that you have run out of something you need to prepare the meal for your family. No?"

"Yes and no," she laughed. "I've run out of milk, but only the cat is disturbed by it." She explained about her Christmas this year, and he chuckled with her.

"Today, then, you can be like me," he said, "alone in a big, empty house while everybody else celebrates their biggest holiday of the year. Perhaps you can stay here with me for a while. We can speak of our families who are not with us this year," he offered, but she caught his furtive glance at the front window. Was he afraid of something, of someone?

"Mr. Feroz, I can tell that something is wrong. Can I help you. . . ?" she began.

He shook his head, refusing to look her in the eyes. "I will be all right, I think. They told me not to open the store on Christmas Day, but I do not believe they will come back today. Such a busy day for most."

"Come back?" she repeated. "Who, Mr. Feroz?" Then, before he answered, she knew. Someone had threatened him because of his faith and his birthplace. "It's the trouble in the Middle East, isn't it?" she asked. "Someone has taken out his frustrations on you."

He nodded, still not looking at her. "I understand

their frustrations," he said then. "But I have done nothing. I came to America to escape the bitter struggle in my homeland. This country has been good to me. Why would I send money to help destroy it? Why would my son, Said, leave his nice job at the university to become a suicide bomber? My family has never agreed with such violence!"

"Mr. Feroz, I am so sorry!" Loraine said. "Did they threaten to hurt you? Perhaps you should call the police."

He shook his head. "They have threatened to burn down the store if I do, to harm my son and his family. They said they know where he lives. I cannot take the risk."

"Who are these people, Mr. Feroz?"

Again, he shook his head. "I do not know, dear lady. There were three of them. They do not live in this neighborhood. They had never been in my shop until two days ago."

They both looked up in alarm as the bell tinkled over the door. Loraine was relieved to see that it was Pastor Ted Hammons.

"May I help you?" Mr. Feroz asked, still a little wary of the visitor.

"It's all right," Loraine whispered. "I know this man."

Ted appeared a little uncomfortable, she thought. Had he given away his winter clothing again? But that couldn't be the reason for his embarrassment. His jeans were topped with a warm, waterproof jacket, and he was wearing gloves. He even had a sock cap perched on his head.

"Hello," he greeted both of them. "What are you doing here on Christmas Day?" he asked Loraine.

"I might ask you the same thing," she countered.

He hesitated. "I guess I might as well confess," he said then, "since you've caught me literally in the act. I'm worried about that mother with the three children who were in the food line the other day. We took Angel Tree gifts to the children and found that they are living in a house the mother inherited from her parents. The good news is that they aren't homeless. But I'm afraid they don't have food. The kids have those big hungry eyes. You know, like you see in those Feed the Children ads on TV."

Loraine felt her heart contract. She and Jack had known some lean years in the early days of their marriage, but their children had never gone hungry. "Can we take them some food?" she asked, already part of the venture in her own mind. Then she felt her face flush as Ted's smile spilled from warm brown eyes to the corners of his mouth.

"Well, I came here to do a little shopping for them. You're welcome to help," he said.

In answer, she grabbed a shopping basket and handed one to him. Quickly, they moved through the market, filling the baskets with potatoes, fruit, cans of vegetables, cereal, and bread. Loraine had thought to add a small ham to the pile, but looking at the meat in its glass case, she realized that Mr. Feroz did not sell the meat of hogs.

Loraine chose the biggest chicken she could find and placed it in her basket. She saw Ted pick up hamburger and a hefty beef roast.

"There," he said, with satisfaction, adding a large bag of cookies to his gleanings. "I think that's all the money I have," he said apologetically.

"Oh, I'll get these," she offered, indicating her own basket. "I just need to add some milk and get some for myself. I almost forgot why I came in here today."

At the register, Mr. Feroz quickly ran the total, then cut it in half. "I, too, will feed the children," he said.

"You don't have to do that, Mr. Feroz!" Loraine exclaimed.

Ted looked at her, then at the shopkeeper. Loraine saw some kind of understanding pass between them.

"Thank you," Ted said. He turned back to add more meat and another bag of cookies to their purchases. Then, picking up two of the grocery bags, he walked out of the store.

Loraine picked up two more and followed him. He placed his bags in the back of a van parked behind her car, then turned for hers. She handed him the sacks, which he placed in the van before going back into the market. She followed, seeing him pick up two more bags and carry them outside.

"Call the police, Mr. Feroz," Loraine urged as she left the market with the last bag and her own jug of milk.

"Come with me. We'll take these to the Perkins family together," Ted invited when they had finished loading the van. "It won't take long. They live just five or six blocks over on the north side of town."

Loraine knew the area, a run-down section of houses. The inhabitants either could not afford to fix them up or were too lazy to do so.

She hesitated. "My son may call from overseas," she began, "and my cat will be missing me, or rather, missing his milk," she added honestly. *Where has my quiet, peaceful Christmas Day gone?* she wondered. Then she realized that the day was still young.

"Put your milk in your car, and get in the van," he insisted. "You're in this deep; you might as well see it through."

Knowing that she really had nothing more important to do, she obeyed.

Chapter 7

As they careened through the wet streets, Loraine held tightly to the armrest. *He drives just like Jack used to,* she thought. She remembered how scared she had been at times, sliding around curves on the wrong side, praying the brakes wouldn't fail when he tailgated, gritting her teeth and hanging on, determined not to admit her fear.

I haven't been in a car alone with a man since Jack died, she realized suddenly, *except for my son and my son-in-law. Relatives.*

"Do you have many relatives in town?" Ted asked, seemingly reading her mind.

"No, I don't have any close relatives left, other than my three children," she answered, eyeing a lamppost flashing by only inches from her face. "I have some cousins in Maine and an aunt in Georgia," she added through clenched teeth. "Slow down!" she cried as the van fishtailed, then righted itself.

"I'm sorry!" he said, easing his foot off the accelerator. "I didn't realize I was scaring you."

"My husband drove just like you when we were teenagers," she said, laughing shakily. "I wouldn't tell him I was scared then, but after we had kids, I learned to speak up for their safety."

"So you're saying I drive like an irresponsible teenager?" he asked indignantly.

"Well. . ."

He burst into laughter. "Don't worry, I'm used to it. My wife used to tell me that all the time. I've tried to do better. Guess I just needed someone to remind me."

"Do you have anyone besides the two sons you mentioned the other night?" she asked, able to concentrate on conversation now that the van was moving steadily at a reasonable speed.

"My dad lives in Oregon with my brother," he said.

"Do you ever visit?" she asked, wondering why he hadn't spent Christmas with some of them.

"Sometimes, but having just taken this new position at the church in October, I didn't want to leave right now," he explained. "My son Craig and his wife are expecting a baby in February, so I'll probably go out then."

"Are both of your sons in Oregon?"

"No, Randy's a geologist working with an oil company in Alaska. But Craig lives in our old house. After Regina died, I felt I had to go where the memories weren't so painful. When this position opened up, I jumped at the chance."

She nodded. "I thought about selling our house when Jack died. I didn't think I could live in that house without him, but my daughters and my son wanted me to keep it. They had never lived anywhere else. Now they only use it as a stopping-off place between travels, and I'm there alone. But I'm glad they talked me out of selling it. I'm content there. It's home. And I like being there when one of them wants to stop off for a while."

"It's time you made a life for yourself, Loraine," he said abruptly, wheeling the van into a driveway, putting it in park, and turning off the motor.

She considered his words, trying to decide whether she should appreciate his concern or resent his meddling.

"I don't mean to meddle," he said then, again uncannily in sync with her thoughts. "But from my own experience, it helps to find closure to that past chapter of life and get on with the next chapter. In our old house,

I kept running into ghosts of Regina. Not literally, of course, but I'd walk into the kitchen and see her stirring something on the stove, or setting the table, or perched on her favorite stool at the cooking bar, leafing through a catalog. I'd see her in the hallway, going into the bathroom or the bedroom, smiling back at me."

At the break in his flow of words, Loraine looked at him and found that he was struggling with emotions the memories had evoked. "I know what you mean," she said gently. "The painful memories mellow over time, but sometimes I still 'see' Jack turning to give some sarcastic comment on the news, looking up at me from the recliner—" Overcome with emotion, she also stopped.

Ted laughed then. "Aren't we a pair, sitting here conjuring up ghosts! Let's go feed these children."

For the first time, Loraine noticed the house in front of them. It was a small brick bungalow. The trim had not been painted in a long time, and a shutter hung crazily from one hinge. The yard had been cleared of fallen leaves, though, and the front stoop was clean-swept, with a pot of frostbitten petunias sitting in one corner. A crayoned wreath of green with red holly berries colored into it hung on the door.

Ted got out of the car, went to the door, and knocked. Ted spoke to the child who answered, and then he waited as she vanished inside the house, leaving the door ajar. Soon a woman appeared in the doorway. Then Loraine saw her open the storm door and come outside to throw both arms around the pastor. She seemed to be crying.

Ted came back to the van and began to unload groceries. Loraine got out to help him. The woman held the door open for them as they carried the bags inside, and the three small children watched wide-eyed.

One of them, a curly haired little blond, reminded her of Beth when she was about six or seven years old—full of curious questions and trusting acceptance of everything from fairy tales to miracles. The other two children might have been her practical ladylike Susan and her impetuous little Jack, who never waited patiently for anything, including food.

Beth, Susan, and Jack, she thought fondly, *not one of them ever went hungry, unless Jack was hungry over there in the desert.* She turned away from her memories of those long-ago children and focused instead on those in front of her. Ted offered them cookies, which the girls took politely and began to munch. The little boy stuffed both of his into his mouth and held out his hand for another.

"Ted," Loraine admonished, "these children may

not have had breakfast yet!" She looked around the kitchen, glad to see that, like the children, it, too, was scrubbed clean. There was no evidence that any food had been prepared or eaten there recently.

"Oh, it's okay," the woman said hurriedly. "They're hungry. With the soup kitchen closed yesterday and today, they haven't had much since the day you saw us there, and certainly no cookies. I'm so grateful for all this," she said then, indicating the bags sitting on her kitchen table. "I don't know how I can ever repay you." The tears began again, and Ted gave her a quick hug.

"Don't worry about it," he said. "Look, I'm putting you on our church's list to receive groceries each week until we can get you some regular assistance. You should have asked long ago."

She nodded. "I suppose I should have, but we've gotten by until recently. My husband's been—" She hesitated, glancing at the children. "—away for a year now," she finished. "Drugs, you know. I've used up what little savings we had. I've even tried to work, but good jobs are scarce, and everyone wants somebody with computer skills that I just don't have. Being a waitress doesn't pay much, and with Calvin only four and no one here to babysit, I've had to pay child care. Dana's very responsible, but I just can't see leaving an eight-year-old in charge of two smaller children."

Ted nodded in agreement. "Can you go back to wherever you came from, Mrs. Perkins?" he asked. "Are there grandparents? Do you have siblings who would help?"

The woman dropped her gaze. "I'm ashamed to go back to Memphis where they all know what's happened," she almost whispered. Again, Loraine saw tears gathering in her eyes.

"It's going to get better now," Ted promised, patting the woman reassuringly on the shoulder. "We have a daycare program at the church. Maybe Calvin could come there if you're working in the daytime. I'm sure we could arrange a 'scholarship' for him. And maybe we can find you some training so you can get a steady job. Oh, by the way, I'd be glad to have the church bus stop by for the children, and you, too, if you wish. I'm sure the girls would like Missionettes on Wednesday nights and our Super Church on Sunday mornings. Calvin will soon be old enough for Royal Rangers, and—"

"We'll let you know," the woman broke into his words.

Loraine felt that Mrs. Perkins was a bit overwhelmed by Ted's many suggestions. *Men can be so insensitive sometimes!* she thought. She supposed he meant well, but the woman might be thinking that the pastor was helping them just to gain members for his church. *Is he?* she wondered, studying him.

"I hope you don't think you have to come just because we've brought you a few groceries!" Ted said then, with that knack he had for reading thoughts. "These things did not come from the church, and you should not feel obligated at all!" he insisted. "Of course, we'd love to have you in our services, but only if you and the children want to come."

"Mama," the dark-haired little girl asked tentatively, "could we? I'd take good care of Calvin and Megan if you can't go with us. Please? Could we go sometime?"

The mother studied the child. "We'll see, Dana," she promised vaguely, then turned back to Ted. "Well, as I said, we'll let you know." Loraine wondered if she was unfamiliar with the church's denomination and wanted to check into it before letting her children get involved. It was something Loraine would have done in similar circumstances.

Suddenly, she saw a wry grin touch Ted's face. "I understand," he said. "But let me assure you, despite what you may have heard, we don't jump over benches or swing from the chandeliers. And we definitely don't handle any snakes!" he added. "I'd be the first one out of there if that happened!"

The woman smiled, but Loraine detected a deep weariness in her eyes. "Thank you, again, for all you've done," she said, "for this wonderful food and for the toys the other night. My children would have had a slim Christmas without them."

"And you need to be putting some of this food into the refrigerator," Loraine put in quickly. "It was nice meeting you." She gave Ted a warning glance and turned to leave.

"I'll be in touch," he promised the woman. "See you, kids!" he added. Loraine was relieved to see that he was following her to the door.

Back inside the van, he turned to her. "You think I came on a little too strong, don't you?" he asked.

Suddenly, Loraine's doubts fled. This man was exactly what he had appeared to be since the day she met him—a warm, caring individual who was rebuilding his own shattered life by helping others rebuild theirs.

"Merry Christmas, Ted," she said, with a smile that said all the nice things she was thinking. "Now take me to my car so I can get home with Tigger's milk and ask him to forgive me for neglecting him."

He returned her smile, started the van, and put it into reverse.

Chapter 8

As they pulled into the parking space behind her Honda, Loraine gasped. Mr. Feroz's front glass had been broken out, and some of the contents of his market lay scattered over the sidewalk.

"Oh, Ted, look!" she exclaimed. "Those men came back to carry out their threats!"

"What threats?" he asked. "Who?"

Suddenly, she saw a flicker of flame back inside the building. "I'll explain later!" she cried. "Do you have a cell phone?" At his nod, she ordered, "Call the police. And the fire department! Call 911!"

As Ted punched in the numbers, Loraine ran into the store. "Mr. Feroz!" she called, dreading what she might find. "Where are you?" There was no answer, and her heart pounded in concern for her neighbor's safety. Had they killed the gentle old man and set the building on fire to cover their crime? She moved frantically through the aisles, calling his name, begging him to answer.

"Loraine?" she heard Ted call from the front of the market. "Where are you? What's going on?"

She ran into the center aisle where she could see the pastor standing in front of the cash register. "Are they coming?" she asked. "The police? The firemen? The EMTs?"

"They're on the way," he assured her. "Have you found him? Is he alive?"

"No. I mean, I don't know. I can't find him!"

She saw Ted tear a fire extinguisher from the wall and begin spraying foam onto the flames that licked greedily at the well-oiled wooden floor.

A groan came from somewhere in the back of the market, and Loraine ran toward it.

"Mr. Feroz!" she cried, discovering the small figure crumpled in a heap behind the meat counter, blood pouring from a gash in his forehead. "Thank God, you're alive!"

"Praise be to Allah!" he said weakly, trying to rise from the floor.

Quickly, she bent to help him, but the old man

shrank back from her. She thought she had read some-where that his religion discouraged close contact with a woman, especially an "infidel." Then Ted was on the other side, guiding him to a seat on a small bench behind the counter. She grabbed a hand towel from the counter and passed it to Ted. "Here," she said, "see if you can stop the bleeding. Is the fire out?" she added.

"No," Ted answered, dabbing at the wound. "But I think it's contained. And help is almost here."

Loraine could hear the distinctive sounds of the emergency vehicles as they turned onto the street and screeched to a halt outside the store. Uniformed men and women raced inside and spread throughout the room. The firemen pulled a hose near the smoldering fire and doused the fire while Ted led the EMTs to Mr. Feroz. Immediately they began to check his vital signs and treat his wounds, while the policemen, with guns drawn, searched the premises.

Soon the officers came to the little huddle of peo-ple around Mr. Feroz. Answering the officers' request for information, Loraine informed them of the threats Mr. Feroz had related to her earlier.

"I begged him to call the police," she said, "but he was afraid of what they might do."

"Well, it looks like they did it anyway," one officer

remarked. "He should have known not to give in to terrorists!"

Terrorists! The word rang in Loraine's mind like an alarm. She had just thought of them as thugs, not terrorists. But she supposed that was what they were, no matter what country they came from or what motivated them. They certainly had succeeded in striking terror into Mr. Feroz's heart and, consequently, into her own.

"They try to burn my market!" Mr. Feroz exclaimed. "They threaten to harm my son! Please, don't let them harm my Said!" he begged, clutching at the jacket of an EMT who was bent over him putting a bandage over the gash in his head. "Please! He is a good boy, a good husband, a good professor at the university. He's done nothing wrong!"

"It's all right, sir," the female EMT soothed, reaching to prepare his arm for a shot.

"Could the male EMT do that?" Loraine questioned. "His religion—"

"Oh, yes. I'd forgotten," the woman said, handing the swab and the needle to the EMT beside her. "The shot will relax him," she explained to Loraine. "He will be okay. His vitals are strong, and he only has the one cut."

"Thank God!" Loraine breathed again.

The woman nodded. "It could have been much worse. But you're a tough one, aren't you, old fellow?" she said to Mr. Feroz. "It takes more than a blow over the head to take you out!"

"Please!" he begged again, looking at the man. "Send someone to protect my Said!"

"We will send word to the police department in that city, sir," an officer promised. "You just relax and let us get you to the hospital."

"No!" the old man protested. "No hospital! I want to go home."

"But, sir, you really should be checked out by a doctor. You might have other injuries," the woman EMT insisted. "We think you're okay, but our resources are limited."

"No hospital!" Mr. Feroz repeated. "I want to go home!"

The woman exchanged glances with Loraine. "I live a couple of doors from him. I can check on him," Loraine offered.

"I can drive him home and check in on him later," Ted added.

The technician nodded. "All right. I suppose that will be okay. Just let us get him to sign this release form, and you can take him home."

"I want everything in here photographed and finger-printed, and I want a guard posted here until that window can be boarded up," Loraine heard one of the policemen order as she left the market behind Ted and Mr. Feroz.

She watched Ted help the old man into the front seat of the van, noting that the rain had stopped and a weak sun was trying to shine through the clouds that still hung over the town. She got into her own car, grateful that it had not been harmed. She reached over and touched the jug of milk, satisfied that it was still cold and unspoiled. Tigger would be happy.

So much for an uneventful Christmas Day! she thought wryly as she put the car in gear, eased out of the parking place, and followed Ted's van down the street. She glanced at the clock on the dash. *Oh, well, it's just past noon. I still have time to enjoy a few hours of unmitigated idleness,* she thought, pulling into her own driveway and turning off the motor.

She could see Ted helping Mr. Feroz from the van two houses down the street and hurried to help.

Mr. Feroz pulled a large, old-fashioned key on a leather cord from inside his loose shirt. He slipped the cord over his head and held the key out to her, dangling from its cord safely above her hand.

Loraine grasped the key and inserted it into the lock on the front door. It turned easily, and the door swung open on silent hinges.

As Ted eased the old man down into the deep sofa cushions, she said, "Point me to the kitchen, and I'll fix you a cup of strong, hot tea." Then she added, "You do drink tea, don't you?"

Mr. Feroz nodded. "But just a glass of water right now, please, dear lady," he said, pointing toward the kitchen. "It is in the refrigerator. I will fix some tea after I rest for a small time." With that, he sank back against the pillow Ted placed behind his head and shoulders. Ted took a brightly colored woven throw from the back of the couch and spread it over him.

Loraine found a glass in the kitchen. She took the bottle of water from the refrigerator and filled the glass slowly, her fascinated glance taking in the Middle-Eastern design of the room and its furnishings. *Casablanca*, she thought. *That's it. This could be a room straight out of Rick's Café Americaine. I wouldn't be surprised if Humphrey Bogart or Ingrid Bergman walked right through the beaded curtain covering that door back there.*

"Isn't Casablanca in Morocco?" she asked herself then. "I'm pretty sure that Mr. Feroz is from Iraq." *Oh, well*, she shrugged, picking up the glass of water and heading back to the living room. *I don't know one Middle Eastern design from another. Maybe I just think it looks like Casablanca. Or maybe his wife was from Morocco.* Maybe someday she would ask him, but this didn't seem like the right time for idle questions.

She held out the glass, and Mr. Feroz struggled to sit up. Ted raised him gently from the pillows and held the glass so he could drink from it.

"I am eternally indebted to each of you," Mr. Feroz said, handing the glass back to Ted, who set it in a small crystal dish on a low table in front of the couch. "My life's blood might have seeped completely away from me there on the floor of my market had you not come along and rescued me."

"I doubt that you would have bled to death, Mr. Feroz," Ted assured him. "But it certainly was better to get you patched up quickly and the police started on an investigation to unearth the culprits who did this to you and your store."

"I pray to Allah that the police will find them soon and put them away where they cannot harm me or my son," the old man said fervently. He sank back against the pillows again and closed his eyes.

"Do you have a pen, Ted?" Loraine asked, picking up a phone book from a nearby table. She took the pen he held out and wrote her phone number on the back of the book. "I'm just two doors away, Mr. Feroz," she reminded him. "If you need me, all you have to do is call."

"Will you call Said and tell him what has happened?" the old man asked. "Tell him I don't want him to come. I just want him to be warned."

"The police said—" she began, but Ted interrupted.

"What is his number?" he asked. "I will call him." He took the pen back and wrote the number Mr. Feroz repeated in a small notebook from his shirt pocket. "We'll get out of here and let you rest now. But I'll be back very soon to check on you," he promised, heading for the door.

Outside, Loraine turned to face the pastor. "Do you think he will be all right here alone?" she asked. "Do you think those men will come back?"

"I'm going to pray hard that they don't," he answered, "but you keep a lookout, and if you notice anything suspicious over here, give me a call." He took a wallet from his back pocket, extracted a business card from it, and held it out to her.

"After I call 911!" she laughed, tucking the card into her jacket pocket.

As Ted drove away, leaving one of those infectious grins behind him like a disappearing Cheshire cat, she suddenly realized how empty the space was where he had been.

"Nonsense!" she told herself, retrieving the jug of milk from her car and carrying it inside. "I'm just tired. I haven't kept a single Christmas tradition, yet I'm as tired as though I'd been up all night cooking and wrapping presents."

She poured milk into Tigger's bowl, set it in the microwave, and punched the buttons.

He came over to watch with wide yellow eyes as the timer clicked off the seconds. *"Maalk!"* he reminded her when the buzzer went off.

She set the bowl on the floor and ran her hand over his soft fur. "Sometimes I almost believe you can talk," she told him fondly.

Sinking into the recliner, Loraine pulled her quilted throw over her. "It's time for that long winter's nap, Tigger," she sighed, already half asleep.

The phone's shrill ring jarred her awake.

"What's going on down at the old Arab's place?" Esther demanded when she answered.

"Oh, Esther, I'm glad you called," she said. "We need to keep an eye out for Mr. Feroz. He was attacked by terrorists. They roughed him up and tried to burn his market!"

"Oh my!" Esther exclaimed. "Terrorists attacking terrorists! What is this world coming to?"

"Esther!" Loraine scolded. "Mr. Feroz has never hurt anyone, at least not in the past twenty years that I've known him. He came here to get away from terrorism, to make a better life for himself and his family, just as my ancestors did at some point in history, and just as you did!"

"*Harrumph!*" Esther objected in disdain. "His son—"

"His son is a professor at some university out West. He's not in training to be a suicide bomber."

"How do you know, Loraine?" Esther asked seriously. "And if he's not, he may be one of those professors the universities seem so intent on coddling these days—the ones who tell their students, 'Kill the infidels!' and raise money for Hamas or Hizballah, or maybe even al-Qaida."

"I know, Esther," Loraine agreed. "Since 9/11 we've all had our suspicions of everything and everybody with any connection to the Middle East. But old Mr. Feroz—" She stopped, suddenly too tired to continue.

"You sound like you need some rest," Esther picked up astutely. "I'll keep an eye out down that way," she promised. "The last thing we need in this neighborhood is an 'incident' over some old Arab. Wouldn't the media love it!" With that, she hung up.

Loraine replaced the receiver on its base and pushed back the recliner. Within minutes she was asleep.

Chapter 9

Loraine struggled upward through the clinging fog of a dream. She was running from a terrorist who was threatening to blow up himself and the soup kitchen. The phone was ringing, and she snatched it up, unsure whether it was real or part of her dream.

"Hello?" she said, her voice thick with sleep.

"Hey! Are you okay?" queried the voice on the other end.

"Jack?" Had the bomber succeeded in blowing her straight into heaven where her husband waited? Then she realized that the voice did not belong to her deceased husband, but to their son. "Jack!" she repeated. "You sound just like your father. Are you all right?"

"I'm fine, Mom," he assured her. "I just wanted to wish you 'Merry Christmas.' I've had a time getting a phone line out of here."

"Oh, Jack, it's so good to hear your voice!" she said, feeling a lump gathering at the base of her throat. She swallowed hard.

"Thanks for the gigantic stocking," he said. "Everything is appreciated and will be put to good use," he promised, "especially the thick, warm socks, and the chocolate that only requires hot water. You know how I hate cold feet and love hot chocolate!"

"I wasn't sure if you needed warm socks or hot drinks over there in the desert," she confessed, glad that she had sent them anyway.

"In the daytime, when that merciless desert sun beams down, we swelter and hunt for shade, but when old Sol sinks into the sea, it gets right chilly. These boots sweat, and when it turns cold, I hunt for dry socks!"

Loraine chuckled, remembering their sledding days. Little Jack—always the first to pull on warm winter clothing and head outside when it snowed—was always the first to retreat inside to sip hot chocolate and toast his nearly frozen feet by the fire.

"Are the girls there?" Jack asked. "I got a package from Susan and a card with photos from Beth, but I haven't talked with either one of them lately."

"No, son," she replied, explaining where they were, and telling him a little about her own futile plans for a quiet Christmas.

He laughed. "Well, you know, Mom, about those 'best-laid plans of mice and men.' I guess that applies to ladies, too."

He sounds like he's right here in the room. If only I could put my arms around him and hold him close for a moment! she yearned. *If only I could keep him safe from any kind of danger!*

"Is it—?" she began, but her voice caught on that lump in her throat. She swallowed and started over. "Is it really bad there, son? Are you in as much danger as the news makes it seem?"

"We never know what to expect," he evaded, "but, hey, don't worry about me, Mom! Just keep praying and trust in the Lord the way you and Pop always taught us to do."

"I pray for you constantly!" she assured him.

"Gotta go," he said then. "Some of the guys are still waiting for their turn on the phone."

Her mind searched for some way to hold him, to keep from breaking this thin connection between them. "I love you, Jack!" she said, wanting at least to touch him with that.

"Love you, too, Mom. Bye," he said and that quickly was gone.

Loraine sat cradling the receiver against her, as though it were her youngest child she was holding against her heart. She breathed a prayer for his safety.

A nasal voice demanded, "If you would like to make a call, please hang up and—"

She placed the receiver back on its base and untangled herself from the throw. *What time is it?* she wondered, noting the darkness outside the patio door.

She moved over to the window and looked out toward Esther's. The lights were on over there, and she could see Esther standing at her window peering out. She waved, then without waiting to see if she waved back, Loraine moved to a window on the other side of the house. *I promised to check on Mr. Feroz,* she recalled, the day's events flooding back into her mind.

The Mitchell place next door was brightly lit, giving its false impression of occupancy and making it almost impossible to see beyond into the darkness. So far as she could tell, there were no lights on in the Feroz house.

Loraine went out onto her front porch and peered into the darkness. *What's going on down there?* she wondered. Were those shadowy outlines people moving around in the Feroz front yard?

Now she could see moving lights, flashlights, she guessed, as newcomers joined the small group. She could hear some shouting, words she couldn't understand. Then she saw a man step up onto the front stoop and begin to paint something on the polished wood of Mr. Feroz's front door.

Loraine left her porch and moved across the yard. She could hear angry voices chanting, and now she could make out the words: "Go back to Iraq! Go back to Iraq! We don't want you here!" As she neared the house, she could read the words splashed across the dark wood in vivid yellow paint: "Arab pig! Get out!"

There was no sign of the old man as the growing crowd trampled his neat front yard and marred his front door. The house was dark, as it was much of the time during the Christmas holidays, the very absence of lights and decorations calling attention to the fact that this was the home of someone different. Suspect.

But he's been here twenty years! she protested silently. *We know him! He brought his wife and child here when his hair and beard were thick and black, and now they are as white as the snow you have trampled into the mud of his yard. He is not a terrorist! He runs the little grocery over on Fourth Street. His son is not a terrorist! He lives in*

Michigan or Wisconsin or somewhere, teaching mathematics at the university.

"Go home, Arab pig!" someone shouted.

"Get out, or we'll drag you out!" another voice threatened. "We'll cut you into pieces like your cousins and friends do to our boys in your godforsaken country!"

Suddenly, Loraine recognized the angry man as the brother of a young man who had been in Susan's high school graduating class. She remembered reading in the paper that the young man had been killed in Iraq. Now this brother had turned his grief and frustration toward this innocent man simply because he was an Arab and followed the Muslim religion. And he had persuaded others to join him. She couldn't be certain in the dim light, but the men gave the impression that they had been drinking alcohol.

Loraine felt the viscous fog of their irrational hatred swirling around her. Fear lumped in the pit of her stomach like cold oatmeal. She had to do something.

Suddenly, without being aware that she had moved, she was standing on the front stoop of Mr. Feroz's home facing the mob. "Go home, yourselves!" she cried. "Leave this poor old man alone! He's done nothing to you!" She grabbed the rag dangling from the back pocket of the painter and began to scrub at the hateful words, smearing the ugly yellow across the once-beautiful polished wood, blurring the words into something as incomprehensible as the mob's unwarranted fury.

The painter snatched the rag from her hands and slapped her across the face with the paintbrush, leaving a wide streak of yellow from her left earlobe to the corner of her mouth. "Arab lover!" he hissed.

The mob cheered and milled about in the yard, as though ready to do something but not yet sure what.

Loraine put her hand to her cheek, feeling the thick paint coagulating there like blood. Fear spread through her. She wasn't an "Arab lover." Nor was she an Arab hater. She simply believed in freedom for everybody. It was what her son was committed to fight for even now. But what could she do against so many?

Then she heard the welcome sirens and saw the flashing lights advancing down the street. Loraine sank down weakly on Mr. Feroz's top step and put both hands over her face, paint and all. When she looked up, the mob had melted away like snowflakes on a warm surface.

She turned to face the old man standing behind her, searching for words to erase the pain the lights from the police cars revealed in his dark eyes, to somehow make amends for what her misguided countrymen had done tonight. "I am so sorry, Mr. Feroz!" she began.

"Praise be to Allah that someone called the police!" the old man said. "I don't know what might have happened if they had not come."

She looked around, wondering what *had* brought the police here just in the nick of time.

A van screeched to a stop behind the police cars, and Ted Hammons got out. *It couldn't have been Ted who called them,* she thought. *It looks like he just found out what was going on over here, or perhaps he has just come by to keep his promise to check on Mr. Feroz.*

Then she saw Esther Cohen standing on the Mitchell's illuminated porch, her cell phone in her hand. Esther's bright brown eyes returned her gaze for several seconds, then she gave a half smile and turned back toward her home.

Epilogue

The idea was born and grew without any encouragement from Loraine. In fact, she resisted it at first. Then, reluctantly, she let go of her last dreams of an idle Christmas and, glancing at the clock, reached for the phone. She would extend her invitations for tomorrow evening, she decided, her excitement growing. What did it matter to any of them that it would be the day after Christmas?

I can put on a pot of green beans and whip up a gelatin salad and a cake tonight, she planned, *and I can bake a sweet potato casserole and some of those rolls from the freezer just before dinner. But what can I do about meat?* There was nothing big enough in her freezer. She had baked that small ham for her own use, but she knew that neither Esther nor Mr. Feroz ate ham. She supposed she should get a small turkey if there were any left.

The stores would be open tomorrow. It was the day everyone makes a mad rush to exchange unwanted gifts and buy leftover Christmas gift items and decorations at huge discounts.

Loraine recoiled from the thought in horror. *I'm not doing any shopping or decorating!* she vowed. There would be no holly on the mantel, no ivy entwining the stair rail. She would simply fix an easy-to-prepare dinner for casual acquaintances with whom she hoped to share a belated Christmas and, perhaps, subtly, the reasons she kept it.

Suddenly, the image of a wide smile lighting brown eyes came into her mind. Well, it really wouldn't take any more effort to prepare for four rather than three, she reasoned—one more place setting at the table, an extra spoonful or two of everything.

"But I'm ordering the turkey baked!" she stated firmly. "And I'm having it sliced!"

O Little Town
of Progress

Chapter 1

The little town of Progress had made no progress at all in the past twenty years, unless one counted the new stoplight at the intersection of Main and Broadway and the McDonald's at the edge of town. Even the big red and white wooden candy canes hanging from the iron posts below the round white globes of the streetlights were the same ones that had decorated the downtown area at Christmas for as long as Mary Martha Sims could remember.

None of that bothered Mary Martha. She hadn't changed much in the past twenty years either, except that she found it somewhat harder now to see where to step off the curb and a great deal more difficult to maneuver the two steps up to Hanley's Drugstore. But she supposed that was to be expected when a body had been on this earth for eighty-three years. Yes, eighty-three last September, she calculated.

Mary Martha stopped in front of Hanley's to catch her breath and try to remember where it was she had intended to go. Absently, she considered the familiar Christmas village displayed in the window and framed by a string of twinkling clear Christmas lights. She couldn't think of anything she needed from the drug-store. After all, the pastor's wife had taken her shop-ping at the grocery just yesterday—or perhaps it had been the day before. Anyway, it wasn't the drugstore or Kroger's that she needed to visit today. She looked around uncertainly, trying her best to remember, as a gust of December wind blustered around her.

Mary Martha drew her sweater closer, annoyed that she had come out once again without her coat. "Good thing I wore my heavy blue sweater rather than that thin pink one," she muttered to herself. *But enough complaining,* she chided herself. *Except for the wind, it's not all that cold. In fact, this is a lovely, sunny day right in the middle of December.*

Mary Martha waved in the general direction of Jayne's Beauty Shop, just in case Jayne was watching from behind the waving Santa in her front window and the blinking colored lights all around it. She made a mental note to tell Jayne how many compliments her new silver hair rinse had brought her at church the Sunday before. She thought the silver gave her dark eyes the bright, sassy look of a bird. A blue jay, she supposed, in this blue dress and sweater.

Sometimes, living in the Sims house, she had felt like a blue jay trying to live in someone else's nest. Jays are usurpers, though. Mary Martha meekly shared what space she had to and retreated to her bedroom or the garden whenever she could do so politely. She and Mother Sims had always been polite to each other.

As she stood watching, the wind whipped the folded awnings over Hanley's front windows and chased a discarded newspaper into the gutter. Then suddenly, her memory clicked into place. She was headed for the newspaper office with the ad written out exactly the way she wanted it and tucked away in her purse. At least that had been her intention. *I hope I didn't leave it on the kitchen table,* she thought as she opened her purse and began to rummage around inside. But it was there, sandwiched between her billfold and her *Pocket Promise Book,* which made her wonder if she had remembered to read her Bible that morning.

"You okay, Mrs. Sims?" A voice interrupted her

thoughts. She turned to find the pharmacist in his cream-colored coat peering at her from the doorway of his shop—actually it was his father's shop. Bill Hanley Jr. now ran the town's only drugstore. Once she had called him Billy, but since the day he came home from college and put on that cream-colored coat, she had been careful to call him Mr. Hanley.

"I'm fine, thank you, Mr. Hanley," she assured him, but she could feel his eyes following her as she slowly made her way down the street. *He needn't worry about me,* she fussed to herself. She was sure if she'd come this far, she could make it two blocks more to the building that housed *The Progress.* She wanted the ad in this week's paper—before she changed her mind.

It would be easy to sell her mother-in-law's cherry dining room suite. Truthfully, she never used it anyway. Olivia couldn't come home except in dire emergencies, and P.T. was too busy with his bank and his wife's social affairs. And even if they were to come, she wondered if she could still put a company meal together at her age.

P.T. and Eleanor always invited her to have dinner at their house on Christmas, the only time she might see her granddaughter and great-grandchildren, if they were able to make the long trip home. This year none of them were coming—her great-grandson and his wife were expecting a baby any day.

Parker wouldn't want her to sell his mother's furniture. He had always insisted that it stay just as she had it arranged in the years before her death in 1994. Of course, he really couldn't insist on anything anymore. He'd had a heart attack and died while sitting at his desk at the bank.

"Mama liked the sofa against that wall," or "Mama always kept that table under the living room window," he would admonish, easing the disturbed item back into its original grooves in the flowered carpet. The memory made her smile.

Parker had been gone three years now. She missed him. But that had not kept her from moving the small, walnut drop-leaf table from the living room to a spot under the kitchen window where it would better meet her needs.

She didn't really mind selling her big black grand piano, either. She rubbed her right hand with the left one. The cold just seemed to gnaw at that bone she had broken sledding in the moonlight on the night Parker had asked her to marry him. Now arthritis had set in, making it impossible for her to play the piano.

Her mind returned to the starlit hill behind Mason's

house, to the joy of young voices calling to each other across the sparkling snow, to the breathtaking thrill of flying down the hill behind Parker on the sled she had borrowed from her brother, Ben.

Even if Parker had admitted to her that his search for a bride had been motivated by the bank's policy of promoting only settled family men, it would have made no difference. She had been certain that her love could melt his cool reserve and make those icy blue eyes sparkle with shared happiness.

Mary Martha thought again of that night on Mason's hill. It had been the last time Parker had ever gone sledding with her, though she had taken the children many times.

She plodded on, thinking about the ad in her purse. She didn't *have* to sell her granny's rocking chair. It didn't take up much room, and she didn't need the money. But if she intended to sell Parker's things, she felt she should be willing to part with something of her own, something that mattered.

How many babies has that chair rocked? she wondered. *Mama and her five brothers. Me and Ben. . .*

Her brother, Ben, was gone now, too, she remembered. It had been a year now—no, maybe two—since the cancer had been discovered. He had lasted barely three weeks. It was the same year locusts killed the Damson plum tree. Ben had so loved climbing that tree, her rag doll under one arm and that mischievous, teasing grin on his face.

Mary Martha hadn't been back to the home place since Ben's funeral. His boys had called to see if she wanted anything from the house, but she had declined. It seemed to be time to get rid of possessions rather than add to them. Her mind went back to the rocking chair and the precious hours she had spent in it rocking Parker Thomas and little Olivia.

She had intended to call her daughter Mary Olivia—after herself and Mother Sims, whose middle name was Olivia. But Parker had insisted on Olivia only. Now she understood Olivia used both names at the convent.

Mary Martha stopped in front of Baker's Ice Cream Parlour, struck by the recollection of sitting with her papa in those same wire-backed chairs at one of those little round tables. *When I finish my errand,* she promised herself, *I'll go into Baker's and treat myself to a strawberry soda.*

She couldn't help chuckling as she thought about how little had changed in the little town. "Progress" really hadn't lived up to its name! *But,* she thought as she stepped carefully off the curb, looked both ways, and crossed the alley, *maybe that's not such a bad thing. Over in Olde Towne everybody's in a hurry to pave paradise and put in a parking lot!* Mary Martha felt for the curb with her foot and stepped up onto the sidewalk.

Chapter 2

Nearby Olde Towne had progressed in the past few years until it was bursting its seams. Charlie Justice liked the changes. The new Chrysler plant and all the related growth—restaurants, schools, subdivisions, and the new hotel right in the middle of downtown—made it an exciting place to be. She and Rick, as owners of the town's first daily newspaper, had been quickly welcomed into the Council for the Arts. They had even been invited to the biggest social event of the year—the Mayor's Christmas Ball at the town's newest and most elegant hotel.

Charlie picked up a paper and began leafing through it. Rick insisted that they subscribe to all the locals and urged her to scan every one of them. He felt this would help them keep track of what was happening in the area, even though the news in the weeklies was too old to be of much value.

Once *The Chronicle* was established, Rick and Charlie planned to buy out the weekly in town. It might take all their combined business and journalistic skills, but Charlie saw no reason why their plan to become *the* newspaper in the area could not succeed.

What they hadn't planned on was Charlie getting pregnant, at least not for a long, long time. She and Rick liked working at the paper together long after their employees went home. A baby simply wouldn't fit well into their busy lives. It was too late to think about that, though. The test was positive; she'd taken it three times. Now she had to find a way to tell Rick.

She didn't have to go through with it, of course. *This is the twenty-first century. Women have control over their own bodies now,* she thought. But the idea repulsed her. The baby growing inside her was part of her, part of Rick, their own flesh and blood—no way could she deliberately destroy their child.

It wasn't a religious thing. She'd been raised by devout Baptist parents who had taken her to every service, but once she left for college, she put all that behind her. Now there was no time in her busy life for religion. It was just—

Will Rick want to get rid of the baby? she wondered. *What if he insists on it?* Charlie felt an unexpected protectiveness rising up inside her. He had made it very clear from the beginning of their relationship that he did not want children for a very long time, if ever. Rick was an only child, born and reared in a staid, affluent section of Philadelphia. Charlie knew he hadn't grown up like she had in a rambling farmhouse with brothers and sisters, knowing the rambunctious joy of pillow fights and the give-and-take of growing up.

Charlie had two of each. Her older brother had been killed in an automobile accident when she was a teenager. It was an old grief but a close one. Bobby, the sibling closest to her own age, had completed law school and joined a big firm in Louisville. She saw him a couple of times a year. One of Charlie's sisters lived on a ranch in Wyoming with her husband and three boys. The other, still single, had moved to Chicago to seek a career in advertising.

Charlie hadn't seen her sisters since the first Christmas after their parents had died—her mom from cancer and her dad, she was convinced, of a broken heart. They had gathered at the home place for Christmas, made plans to sell the farm, and then gone their separate ways. They kept in touch by phone and e-mail but rarely saw each other.

I really wouldn't mind having several children, she thought, *someday.* In the crowded years of sharing everything, wearing hand-me-downs, she never thought she would someday miss being part of a big family. Now she wished they all lived close enough to gather for holidays and share the special events in all their lives—the graduations, weddings, births.

Quickly, Charlie pushed her chair back from the desk and put her head between her knees. If only this miserable nausea, this tendency to faint would pass! She wondered if this disoriented feeling was something like what her mother described as "a swimming in the head." Toward the last, when she was on strong pain medication for the cancer, she had commented, "My head feels just like it did when I was pregnant."

Charlie supposed she really should make an appointment with her doctor. But then she would have to face the fact that this was real—she was going to be a mother. She pictured the life her own mother had lived, staying at home to raise her family. Her mother had seemed happy, never complaining, but it made Charlie feel tied down just thinking about it.

Were they doomed to become the kind of parents whose crying baby disrupts an important meeting or much-anticipated performance? She'd seen that happen many times to parents who had no close family or friends to babysit. They certainly didn't have anyone. And they couldn't afford to hire a sitter very often.

Then a new thought hit her. How could they afford to hire someone to do the countless tasks she performed each day for the paper? She was responsible for all the bookkeeping: the payroll, the taxes, the accounts receivable and payable. She did the social page, the obits, and the editorials. Then there were the interviews, the pictures, and the writing of features.

Would she end up interviewing celebrities with a baby strapped to her back like a papoose? Would her crowded office be forced to accommodate a playpen and toys? Would her concentration be interrupted every few minutes by the demands of a fretful baby?

This so-called morning sickness seems to last all day some days, and this appears to be one of those days, she thought wearily, reaching for another paper.

Chapter 3

The chimes of the tall stone church behind her reminded Mary Martha Sims that it was eleven o'clock and she only had a block to go. She couldn't help letting her eyes wander across the street to the small brick church where she and Ben had gone to Sunday school and she and Parker had said their wedding vows. After that, they had attended Parker's cold stone church every Sunday morning. Eventually, he had insisted that she move her membership there.

Parker would be upset if he knew she was thinking about moving her membership again, this time to the little church down the street from their house, the one he had called "holy roller" because they clapped their hands and accompanied their singing with a lively piano and bass guitar.

On those frequent Sunday evenings when Parker had been too busy with his accounts to attend church, she had taken the children there. And, though she never asked them not to, neither of them ever said a word to their father or grandmother about where they had been. She knew her son's loyalty likely had been to youth group festivities, but Olivia had loved the worship services and had not wanted her father to forbid them to go. When Mary Martha had accepted Jesus Christ as her Savior during one of the summer revivals, Olivia had gone forward, too.

Mary Martha had always suspected that it was Collin Davis marrying the oldest Harris girl that sent Olivia into the convent when she was nineteen years old. It was hard to imagine that Olivia had been at the convent for more than forty years. Thankfully, her letters indicated that she was content with the life she had chosen.

P.T. had his bank in Suttonville. She was grateful for the phone call she received every Sunday afternoon at 3:30—as punctual as an alarm clock. P.T. was fifty-nine years old and definitely his father's son, but he didn't want the Sims house or its furnishings. Perhaps that was because of the somber childhood he'd spent there. Or perhaps it was because of his wife, Eleanor, who wanted a newer and finer house every few years.

Mary Martha sighed again. She had lived in the same house for more than sixty years, ever since she and Parker had come back from their weekend honeymoon and moved in with his mother.

She had dreamed of a place of their own, perhaps a small Cape Cod cottage with an apple tree for climbing out back and a white fence around the yard to protect the children. She had pictured holly bushes under the windows, with their red berries lending joy to the place when winter had drained all color from the yard. Instead, she got Mother Sims who managed to drain all the color from their lives. She had mentioned her dream to Parker only once.

"My grandfather built this house," he had responded in that tone his mother used when Mary Martha was straining her patience to the limit. "My dear, we always use the crystal vase with the roses!" or "Oh, no, dear! The white linen cloth, please!"

Finally, she had resigned herself to life in the tall, dark house under the ever watchful eyes of her mother-in-law. Later her faith had enabled her to endure without resentment, though she often longed for a better atmosphere in which to bring up her children.

Even Christmas in that house had been a cold, formal affair, she recalled, though she had tried her best to make it a pleasant time for the children. She had insisted on P.T. and Olivia being allowed to hang their home-made ornaments on the tree, though at some point during the holidays she would find that they had been moved to the back where they wouldn't show.

Mary Martha sat down to rest for a minute on the green wooden bench at the bus stop. Suddenly smiling, she recalled the pleasant trips she and the children had made on the city bus to the park. They went often to give the children a chance to laugh aloud without giving Grandmother Sims a headache or to run and play without endangering her formal garden. In bad weather, they sometimes opted to ride the bus along its entire route and back again just to escape the cold, dark house and the watching eyes for a while.

A few days after Parker's funeral, she had replaced Mother Sims's portrait over the piano with a Paul Sawyier print of sheep gracing peacefully along a country lane. She had kept the picture in her bedroom since Ben had given it to her for her birthday one year. He had framed it himself. She never had said a word to Ben against her husband or his mother, but Ben had known.

She didn't hate Mother Sims. She really didn't. She never believed the woman meant to be unkind to her and her children. It was just that Mother Sims had been raised as an only child by austere parents and had been widowed young. She had raised her son the same way, with strong moral values and rigid conformity to propriety. As the years passed, Mary Martha had grown to understand her mother-in-law, but that hadn't made living with her any easier.

Parker would not have liked her relegating Mother Sims to the attic with her face to the wall. But Parker was gone, and now when she dusted or ran the sweeper, she no longer felt those condemning eyes following her every movement.

Mary Martha glanced across the street at the First National Bank where Parker had spent his days. She could almost see him emerging from the wide front door, with its tasteful real pine wreath tied with a deep red velvet bow to mark the season. His black umbrella would be over his arm, and he would stop to center his hat firmly on his head before walking home.

Parker's bank. Parker's house. Parker's family heritage. These were the things that had given her husband his identity and had engulfed hers. Sometimes she had felt that, if she hadn't stood where his shadow gave her substance, she might fade away completely.

Progress was a part of her identity as well. She had memories of her childhood and family that went beyond the years of her marriage.

Mary Martha had lived in the little town since the day she was born, and she had no intention of living anywhere else. P.T. and Eleanor had asked her to "come stay awhile" with them in Suttonville. But she had already decided to move into one of the senior citizen apartments when she could no longer get by on her own. They were bright and attractive, and the church ran a bus over there. They weren't cheap; the added expense would strain her part of Parker's pension and her social security allotment. But Mary Martha was sure she could manage. Her friend Dolly Farney had lived in the senior apartments for four or five years now, and she liked it just fine.

Mary Martha stopped outside the double wooden doors that bore the inscription *THE PROGRESS*, ESTABLISHED 1892. She pushed into the newspaper office.

Chapter 4

Charlie Justice pulled her small white sports car into one of the parking spaces around the center square of new town houses. She got out, picked up the stack of newspapers she had brought home to read, and locked the car. She inserted her house key into the door of the one she and Rick had made a down payment on nearly a year ago and opened the door.

This will be our first Christmas in our new home, she thought. She could see almost the entire space from the entry, except, of course, the master bedroom and bath hidden around a landing at the top of the stairs on her left. To her right was the galley-type kitchen, and straight ahead was the L-shaped living room that wrapped around into a dining space that backed into the serving bar of the kitchen. *Neat, compact, practical, yet attractive,* she approved. *The place has shaped up rather nicely, if I do say so myself,* she thought with satisfaction, taking in the muted blues and grays of the carpet, wallpaper, and paint with unexpected accents of green.

A green marble fireplace surrounded by overflowing floor-to-ceiling bookshelves dominated the far wall, shared by both living and dining space. It had been one of the deciding factors in their buying this place. They both had so many books! On the few occasions when they had entertained, even with candles on cloth-draped card tables, the space had looked charming in the soft light.

With the moving expenses, down payment on the town house, and costs of setting up the paper, they had little money left for furniture. They had the necessities covered, but the rest would have to wait. They were determined not to go back to Rick's dad for help until they could repay the loan he had given them to get started. The dining area would remain empty until they could afford something nice on their own.

At least that had been the plan—until lately. Rick was saying that they really needed to entertain some influential people during the coming holidays. Their makeshift tables, even with the best white cloths and napkins, wouldn't do for a dinner like that.

Charlie needed dining room furniture, and she needed it quickly. But where would she find something nice for a price they could afford?

Suddenly, for the first time, she felt smothered, trapped by the small space. *There is not enough room here for the kind of dinner Rick would like to give this Christmas,* she thought. *There's not enough room for a dining room suite like the one we need.*

Charlie tossed the papers onto the coffee table, went to the refrigerator, and poured a glass of orange juice. Then she came back to sit on the sofa, sipping the juice and leafing through the papers she had brought home with her. She had read through the dailies at the office, but the nausea had been overwhelming. Finally, she'd given up and headed home, bringing the weeklies with her.

It was while she was looking through the classifieds that she saw the ad from the nearby town of Progress. The ad described a cherry table, eight chairs, buffet, and china cabinet—all for a very reasonable price. Charlie circled the ad with red marker. But would all that furniture fit into their space? She really needed to see it and do some measuring before she got her hopes up.

Even if the furniture fit, there was certainly not

enough room in their little town house for a baby! "What am I going to do?" she whispered, tossing the paper on top of the stack on the table. She was sure that Rick would be appalled by the prospect of moving again so soon. And what about their purchase agreement? They were locked in. Unless they could sell the property quickly, they would be stuck with two house payments for longer than they could afford.

The sound of a key in the front door scattered her thoughts. She looked up to see Rick come into the entry.

"Hey, sweetheart!" His smile began at his wide mouth, just above the neat honey blond beard, and traveled to light up his deep blue eyes. *Rick's not really a handsome man*, she thought for surely the thousandth time since she had met him in the research section of the college library, *but what eyes!*

"I've been trying to reach you. You didn't have your phone turned on again, Toots," he said, using the nickname he had given her in college. She had always found it amusing—until today. She really didn't feel like a "Toots" right now.

"What are you doing home in the middle of the day?" he asked. "Shirking your responsibilities as co-owner of the best and busiest newspaper in town?"

Then his smile disappeared. "Are you all right?"

"I'm okay, Rick," she answered, averting her eyes from his piercing gaze. What she wanted to say was, *"No, I'm not all right! I'm pregnant, and all our plans are ruined!"* She wanted to feel his comforting arms around her, to hear him say, *"A baby? Hey, sweetheart, don't worry! We'll make it. Everything's going to be all right."*

"Rick, I. . . ," she began.

"What's this?" he interrupted, picking up the paper with the circled ad from the coffee table. He read the part she had marked, then gave a low whistle. "Good price! I think we might even be able to swing it with the way ad sales have been going. That Jason is a real go-getter! I am eternally grateful that we hired him." He read the ad again. "It sounds huge! Will it fit? I'd love to have it here before the holidays, but you'd better do a little measuring before you make any commitments."

He walked to the bookshelves, opened one of the doors that hid the bottom two shelves, and took out a camera bag. "Well, furniture placement is your department," he said cheerfully. "I just dropped by to get this camera with the zoom lens. I have to cover the swearing in of the new city council this afternoon." He dropped a kiss on the top of her head and was out the door before she could organize her thoughts.

Charlie drew a shaky breath, fighting another bout of nausea. She had been so close to telling him! Now he was expecting her to check out that dining room suite. They needed it for the Christmas entertaining, but if they bought it, there would be even less room for all the paraphernalia a baby required.

She could understand Rick's reluctance to start a family so soon. She agreed with him. He still had at least a semester of school to finish before he had his master's degree in hand. She hadn't even started hers. The plan had been for her to enroll once he finished. Would she ever get it done once she was bogged down in diapers and formula and potty training? Would she become a copy of her own mother, living her life for her children, never having a life of her own?

Charlie snatched up the discarded paper, rummaged in a kitchen drawer for a tape measure, stuffed it into her shoulder bag, and grabbed her car keys.

Chapter 5

Mary Martha Sims set the teakettle on the stove and then stopped to listen. Was that the doorbell? The tinny sound of the old manual bell hardly penetrated all the way back to the kitchen anymore. Or was her hearing beginning to go?

Turning on the burner, she headed down the hall toward the front door and peeked through the clear petals of a tulip etched into the frosted glass. All she could see was the lower half of a pair of legs in blue pants that ended with navy, low-heeled shoes. The toe of one shoe was impatiently patting the concrete porch.

Mary Martha unlocked the door and narrowed her eyes as she scrutinized the young woman before her. With her matching pants and sweater, dark hair cut almost like a man's, and faintly lipsticked mouth set in an impersonal smile, Mary Martha doubted that she would be the type to need or even want Granny's rocker. She glanced at the short, square hands. Not likely the hands of a pianist. She must have come for the dining room suite. Mary Martha opened the door.

"I'm here about your ad," Charlie explained, holding up the paper with Mary Martha's ad circled in red. "Would it be convenient for me to see the cherry dining suite?"

Mary Martha stared at her for a moment, then extended her right hand. "Mary Martha Sims," she said.

"Sorry! Charlie Justice," the young woman responded, taking Mary Martha's hand, her grin this time wide and infectious.

"Come in," Mary Martha invited, leading the way down the hall to the dining room, then stepping aside for Charlie to enter.

"Why, it's exquisite!" Charlie breathed, reaching out to touch the polished wood, which glowed in the soft afternoon light slanting through tall, lace-covered windows. Then she added, "It may be a bit large for our space. May I measure?"

Mary Martha nodded as Charlie took a measuring tape, a pen, and a notebook from her shoulder bag and began to measure and make notes.

"The piano's in the parlor, if you'd care to measure it," Mary Martha added, a bit sarcastically.

"Thank you," said Charlie. "But neither of us play, and our home is really quite—"

The shrill whistle of the teakettle cut her off. Mary Martha hesitated. She didn't want to leave a stranger prowling about her house while she went to the kitchen. "If you're finished, come with me, please," Mary Martha said, hurrying Charlie down the hall before she could protest. She removed the kettle from the burner and added a teabag. "The rocking chair is there in the corner," she volunteered.

"Oh—I'm sorry—I was only interested in the dining room suite," Charlie answered, looking nervously around the room. Then she put her hand to her face and reached out for the back of a ladder-back chair to steady herself.

Mary Martha was at her side instantly, leading her to the rocker and easing her into it.

Charlie laughed shakily. "I'm so sorry," she muttered. "I'll be fine now." Her voice trailed off as she sank into the chair. Her face was pale, and perspiration had broken out across her forehead.

Mary Martha pushed Charlie's head down between her knees. "Keep your head down a few minutes. I'll fix you a nice cup of hot tea." Surprisingly, Charlie obeyed. When she finally raised her head, Mary Martha saw that she rested it against the ruffled cushion suspended from the chair's back posts.

"I fainted every time," Mary Martha said, handing her the fragile moss rose saucer holding the steaming teacup. "And the nausea! Oh my!"

Charlie looked up at her, misery plain in the wide blue eyes.

Mary Martha smiled. "I know exactly how you feel, Char—" Mary Martha stopped. The name sounded so ridiculous.

"It's Charlene," the young woman clarified as though she had read Mary Martha's mind, "but I only use it on checks and business papers." She sipped from her cup, then laid her head back against the cushion, closed her eyes, and began to rock gently. "Nice chair," she murmured.

"How far along are you, Charlene?" Mary Martha asked softly.

Charlie opened her eyes, seemed to struggle with a decision, then answered. "Two months, more or less."

"The sickness likely will pass in another month," Mary Martha said. "Mine did." *Except for the last one,* she remembered. She had been sick the whole seven months, and then the baby had been stillborn. Parker had said there must have been something wrong with the baby, and it was for the best.

She was sure that Parker loved their two children, in his own way. He was proud of their accomplishments and kept their photographs on his desk at the bank. But she had suspected that Parker hadn't wanted this last baby. Babies were a lot of trouble.

She hadn't burdened Parker with her grief, and she certainly wasn't going to worry Charlene with it now! "Drink your tea before it gets cold," she said instead.

Charlie sat up and sipped at the tea. "I'm so sorry to inconvenience you," she apologized again. "And I really must be going." Nevertheless, she made no attempt to move. Instead, she sipped her tea and rocked gently back and forth in Mary Martha's granny's rocker.

Somehow, she looks right in that chair, Mary Martha thought. *Or maybe it's just knowing that she's expecting.* Rocking chairs were made for mothers and babies, after all. There's just something about a rocking chair, something warm and soothing, something eternal to pass on from one generation to the next.

"This is a lovely old house," Charlene commented. "Have you ever considered adding a window, maybe even a skylight, here in the kitchen to brighten things up?"

A skylight? Mary Martha thought, her shoulders tightening with resentment. *Who does she think she is coming in here and telling me how to change my house?* Then she let her shoulders sag with resignation. The house never had been hers, not even during these past three years when she had lived in it alone with her name on the deed. *It always has and always will belong to Mother Sims,* she realized, *at least in my mind.*

"I probably would tear out that wall and open the kitchen right into the dining room, with maybe a serving bar to separate them," Charlene continued, sipping her tea and rocking contentedly. "Or at least join the two rooms with a wide arch. And I think I'd replace those dark cabinets, or maybe paint them white or a nice sunlight yellow."

Mary Martha looked at her with one raised eyebrow. It was the look Olivia had called her "I've had enough of this nonsense!" look.

Charlene sat up abruptly and placed both feet solidly on the floor to stop the rocker. "I'm so sorry!" she said. "I don't know what got into me! It's a beautiful house just the way it is. It reminds me of my husband's parents' home in Philadelphia—dignified and elegant. I'm not sure why I presumed to remodel it for you!"

Mary Martha smiled. "That's all right, Charlene,"

she assured her. "I've always thought the house was dark and intimidating. It reflects my mother-in-law's taste, not mine. I've often longed to remodel it myself, but while my husband was alive, he wouldn't hear of it. By the time it came to me, I guess I just felt that it wasn't worth all the trouble for the little time I might have left on this earth."

"I wish we could have bought an old house that I could remodel," Charlie said. "If you ever decide you want to tackle this one, give me a call. I'd love to help." She fumbled in her purse, then handed Mary Martha a business card. "And I'd like to do a feature article on this place sometime in the New Year, if that would be agreeable with you."

Mary Martha looked at the card. "We'll see, dear," she stalled. "And are you interested in the dining set?"

"I like it very much, and I think my husband will, too," Charlie said standing up at last. "I'm just not sure it will fit into our tiny town house. Could you hold it for a couple of days while I take these measurements and work with them? I promise I'll get back with you right away."

Mary Martha nodded and turned to follow Charlie to the front door.

As Mary Martha opened the door, Charlie stuck out

her hand. "It was nice meeting you," she said. "And I do hope it will fit—maybe without the china cabinet."

Mary Martha nodded again. "Yes, I could break up the set if necessary. I'm sure the cabinet would sell alone." *If not, I can keep it,* she thought, *or give it to someone.* She didn't think Eleanor would want it, but her granddaughter or one of her great-grandchildren might.

"I'll let you know," Charlie called back as she got into her car.

Mary Martha shut the door and went back to the kitchen. She switched on the overhead lights. *It is dark in here,* she admitted. *But a skylight?* She chuckled then, thinking how Parker would have reacted to the suggestion, or even worse, what Mother Sims would have said. For a moment, the idea was tempting.

Maybe a big picture window there overlooking the back garden, she mused, *where the morning sun can come spilling through onto the golden poplar floor. Or maybe double glass doors opening onto a deck like that lovely one P.T. had built for Eleanor just before she decided they should move again to a more "suitable" neighborhood.*

"I'd love sitting on a deck on sunny mornings, sipping tea, listening to the birds, watching moss roses open in the garden," she said aloud. Mother Sims never would have moss roses in her formal gardens.

"An inelegant flower," she had deemed the lovely little blossoms that had always been among Mary Martha's favorites. Once she had tried growing some in a pot in her bedroom upstairs, but they had died for lack of sunlight. *I could have pots of them on a deck without even disturbing Mother Sims's precious formal beds,* she thought longingly.

If her brother were still alive, he'd build her a deck. Perhaps she could get one of his sons or some other carpenter to do it.

Nonsense! she scolded. *I'm eighty-three years old! I've lived in this dark, old house for more than sixty years. It's foolish to think about changing it now.*

She hoped Charlene would be able to use the dining room suite, though. Suddenly, she felt the need to get that big dark furniture out of the house, to make room, to unclutter, to lighten things up.

Chapter 6

Back in her office, Charlie Justice worked furiously for the rest of the afternoon, taking time out only to deal with recurring bouts of nausea and threats of fainting. At 4:00 p.m., she turned off her computer.

"Ellen, I'm going home!" she called to their jack-of-all-trades assistant in the front office. "See you tomorrow!"

Ellen looked up from her cluttered desk, her glasses pushed up into her black curls, a smear of White-Out on her dark skin below her right cheek bone. "Are you okay, Charlie?" she asked, a frown creasing her forehead. "Obviously, you haven't been feeling well lately. Maybe you ought to see a doctor. You know this flu has been going around, and there's a virus. . ."

Charlie read genuine concern in the woman's dark eyes and smiled at her warmly. "You are very astute, Ellen," she said. She had tried her best to hide her symptoms. "I don't think I'm coming down with anything. Maybe it's just fatigue. If I'm not better by next week," she promised, "I'll call the doctor. Have a nice evening!" And, with that, she was out the door, into her car, and heading for home.

Once there, she changed into a comfortable old sweat suit, fixed a hot cup of lemon tea, and took the measuring tape and her notes out of her shoulder bag. She measured the L-shaped room. *L-shaped, upside down,* she thought, scribbling notes, then measuring again.

She thought the table and chairs would fit in the middle of the room, and the buffet along the wall shared by the living and dining areas. *Whether we will have enough room to walk around them, I don't know!* she thought. There definitely wasn't going to be room for the china cabinet, but she could keep her best dishes in the buffet. Mrs. Sims had indicated that she was willing to sell the set without it.

I like Mrs. Sims, she mused. *She must be eighty, and still she appears to be alert and in control of her life. I hope I'm like that when I'm her age!* Then she laughed aloud.

I'm not even in control of my life right now! she reminded herself.

Rick had said they probably could afford the dining set, and she knew he wanted it in place for the holidays. Should she call Mrs. Sims and say they'd take it? Charlie decided she would feel better if she talked it over with Rick first. And there still was the issue of the baby.

I have to tell him! she thought. The purchase of the dining set—all their decisions from now on—would be impacted by the fact that they were going to have a baby. Certainly, *her* life would be changed completely.

Will I be a good mother? she wondered suddenly. Her own mother had been wonderful, even if, at times, she had felt smothered by her loving concern. Did she have it in her to put the needs of a child above all of her own wants and needs? She didn't know. All she knew for sure was that she wasn't ready for that kind of responsibility, not yet.

A wave of longing swept over her. *If only I could talk it all over with Mom! Would she be shocked by the very unmotherly reactions of her youngest daughter?* She'd never know.

She had been there for all of her sister Sarah's three difficult but much-wanted pregnancies. She supposed she could call her, but Charlie doubted that her oldest sister would be able to identify with someone who didn't want her baby. *She's so like Mom!* she thought. *And it's not that I don't want my baby. I just don't want it yet!*

That didn't change the fact that the baby would arrive in another seven months or so. She would be like all those other mothers at gatherings who could talk of nothing more exciting than how many ounces of formula their little darlings consumed, how many teeth they had cut, how clever they were about learning to talk or to walk or to potty train.

"I will not!" she said aloud. "I will not let this baby rule my life!" As soon as Rick got home, she would tell him. Then she would insist that they go ahead with their plans to buy the dining room suite and entertain for the holidays. The coming baby and its needs would just have to fit in around all that as well as with all the other parts of their busy lives.

At the sound of a key inserted into the front door lock, her heart sank. He was home! It was time. She took a deep breath and swallowed hard, trying to arrange the words of her disturbing announcement on her tongue.

"Get your duds on, Toots!" Rick sang out when he saw her. "We're going to the Mayor's Christmas Ball!"

Charlie was alarmed. She had totally forgotten that the ball was tonight. "But, Rick, I have—"

"No 'buts' about it, babe," he interrupted. "This is one invitation that cannot be turned down. I've worked too hard to get it! And I know you were about to say that you have nothing to wear, but that red velvet dress you wore to Mom and Dad's anniversary party will be perfect. I hope I can still fit into my wedding tux."

Charlie let her breath out in a long sigh, swallowing the news she had been on the verge of sharing. The last thing she wanted to do tonight was go to some formal political affair. She wanted to stay right here and tell her husband they were going to have a baby. She wanted it all behind her. Looking at the excitement shining in her husband's eyes, though, she knew she couldn't spoil it for him. At least the nausea usually bothered her less in the evenings.

"I've got the first shower!" she told him, heading for the stairs.

Chapter 7

"We're so glad you could come to our Senior Saints Christmas dinner, Mrs. Sims!" the pastor's wife said. "Sit down here, and I'll get you a plate."

Mary Martha sat down in a folding chair at a round table covered with a white cloth and decorated with a large pot of poinsettias in its center. Each of the eight places at the table was set with a little basket of candies, a paper napkin of red poinsettias, and silverware.

Stainless ware, she corrected silently. *No one uses silver anymore.* That didn't bother her, though. She had hated polishing Mother Sims's silver. Mother Sims had always done the cooking, assigning Mary Martha the more menial tasks, things she apparently thought her incompetent daughter-in-law could handle. She hadn't even been allowed to wash the good dishes after she broke a soup bowl from the best china early in her marriage. Of course, there was a maid who came in to help with the heavy cleaning two days each week.

Soon after Parker's funeral, Mary Martha had packed up most of the "good" silver and given it to P.T. In addition to the table service for twelve, there had been a lovely tea set she would have given to Olivia had she had a home of her own.

Her daughter-in-law seemed pleased with the gift, for once, oohing and aahing over the elegant pattern and the obvious quality of the silver. She even noted with satisfaction the prestigious name of the manufacturer.

"Here you go!" Mrs. Tanner, the pastor's wife, said, placing a filled plate in front of her. Mary Martha recognized the usual turkey, dressing, and cranberry sauce, with other interesting mixtures heaped around them.

"Would you like iced tea or hot coffee?" Mrs. Tanner asked.

"Tea, please," Mary Martha answered, spearing a bite of dressing with her fork and combining it with cranberry sauce.

The pastor's wife patted her on the shoulder. "I never drink coffee in the evenings, either," she approved. "I'll be right back with your tea."

Mary Martha shrugged off her irritation at the woman's unconscious patronizing. She was a kind woman who was always offering to do some favor for her. When she had taken her to the grocery this week, she had urged her to come tonight, reminding her that the church bus stopped right at the end of her front walk.

Mary Martha often took the bus to church on Sunday and Wednesday nights, when it was too dark outside to walk the short distance to the church. Only recently, though, at her friend Dolly's insistence, had she begun to participate in some of the congregation's social events.

She was glad she and Dolly had become friends. They had known each other in school, but it wasn't until they met up again here at the church, both widows, that they had become real friends. They were as different as two people could possibly be, but she enjoyed Dolly's sarcastic comments on everything around them, her enthusiastic optimism.

She put the dressing and cranberry sauce into her mouth and swallowed. *Delicious!* she thought in surprise. *Almost as good as Mother Sims's corn bread dressing.* Despite her faults, she had to admit that Parker's mother had been an excellent cook.

Finding that she was hungry, she explored other

offerings on the plate. *Dolly would love this sweet potato casserole,* she thought, scanning the crowd for her missing friend. *Where is she?*

"Hello, Mrs. Sims!"

Mary Martha looked up into the eager smile of a man she recognized as a local Realtor. He had done business with Parker at the bank and was ten years younger than she. He and his wife had once come for dinner, an evening she had thought would never end. She remembered hearing that his wife had died a few years ago and he had remarried—a considerably younger woman. She couldn't remember his name, but it would come to her. *Probably tomorrow,* she thought wryly, *when I no longer need it.*

"Good evening," she answered casually.

"Tom Winters," he supplied, pulling out the chair beside her and taking a seat. "When are you going to let me sell that big old monstrosity of a house for you?" he asked, cutting right to the purpose for his sudden friendliness. "I could get you a great price! Those old Victorians are in demand again. And no wonder, not too many of them left, originals like yours, anyway."

"Mr. Winters," Mary Martha said, buttering her roll, "I am not interested in selling my house." She knew she used the possessive pronoun loosely. It would never be her house. But she was sure the Realtor knew her name was on the deed. "I've lived there for more than sixty years, and I suppose I'll die there," she added. "Then you and your competitors can fight with my son over it."

Somehow, lately, I've learned to speak my mind, she thought proudly, *and most of the credit for that should go to Dolly.* The woman was about as tactful as the proverbial bull in a china shop but painfully honest. *Perhaps she has rubbed off a little on me,* she thought. *If only I'd had Dolly's influence in my life years ago.*

"But, Mrs. Sims, I could get you a great price!" the Realtor repeated. "You must rattle around in that big old place all by yourself. I could find you something smaller, something cozy and easy to keep. Let me get you an offer, and—"

Mary Martha carefully placed her knife across the edge of her plate and turned to look him squarely in the eyes. She could almost see the dollar signs dancing. "Mr. Winters," she said firmly, as though he were hard of hearing, or maybe a little slow, "let me make this perfectly clear: I—am—not—interested."

He met her unblinking stare for a moment, then dropped his gaze, pushed back his chair, and left the table.

"Merry Christmas!" Mary Martha muttered, taking

a bite of the buttered roll.

"Oh, Merry Christmas to you, dear Mrs. Sims!" the pastor's wife gushed, placing a tall glass of tea in front of her. "It's sweetened. I hope that's all right. You're not diabetic, are you?"

Mary Martha shook her head no. *I'm not diabetic, and I'm not completely senile,* she thought. Then, realizing contritely that the woman only meant to be nice, she added, "Happy New Year, my dear."

Mrs. Tanner patted her on the shoulder again and moved away to greet some new arrivals. Among them, Mary Martha spotted Dolly Farney. She waved to her and motioned to the seat beside her. Dolly waved back and started to work her way through the crowd.

"Hey!" she said when she reached the table, removing her coat and neck scarf and draping them over the back of the chair the Realtor had just vacated. "Glad you could make it! Did you ride the bus? Ours was late." She dropped heavily into the chair.

Mary Martha suppressed a shudder as she took in the purple dress encasing Dolly's plump body. *It's exactly the shade of her hair! If only I could convince Dolly to go to Jayne and allow her to create something more suitable!* she thought as someone placed a filled plate in front of Dolly.

"Mmmmm, this is good!" Dolly exclaimed around a mouthful of sweet potato casserole. "Pecans. Cornflakes. Pineapple. What else? If I still cooked, I would want this recipe!"

Mary Martha pushed back her half-empty plate and sipped her tea.

"Aren't you going to finish your food?" Dolly asked. "You're thin as a bird! I know you don't eat right, there in that big old house by yourself. After Mr. Farney died, I got so I hardly bothered to fix a meal. Now I make my own breakfast, and the Senior Center provides lunch and dinner. It's pretty good most of the time." She chuckled, waving one hand at her ample middle. "You can tell I'm not going hungry!"

Mary Martha smiled noncommittally, considering the tray of desserts being offered by a teenage waiter. She selected a small piece of cheesecake topped with cherries and saw Dolly reach for a huge serving of some decadent-looking chocolate concoction.

"What a way to go!" Dolly said, rolling her eyes. Mary Martha laughed aloud. She was glad she had come. Dolly was right. She needed to get out more.

"You really should consider selling that old place and moving out to the Senior Center with me," Dolly said. "You never liked that house anyway, and it must be hard to keep. At the Senior Center, they do all the heavy cleaning for us. And there's always something going on—games, entertainment, or just visiting with other residents. I haven't been bored or lonely a day since I moved in," she added, poking a forkful of chocolate into her mouth.

Mary Martha took a bite of her cheesecake, chewed, and swallowed, envying, for the first time, the freedom and camaraderie Dolly had found in her new lifestyle. She and Parker had never had close friends— mostly acquaintances, business associates, people to impress with their formal dinners. Mother Sims had held teas for her garden club and entertained her bridge club.

Once, Mary Martha remembered, she had asked someone home for lunch, a nice girl she had met on the city bus, back before she had children. They had talked several times and had a lot in common. Mother Sims had been polite during the visit, but after the girl left, she had enlightened her errant daughter-in-law about the dangers of picking up strangers. She also mentioned that it was inconsiderate to invite guests to someone else's house. Mary Martha never made that mistake again.

"Of course, I don't own it," Dolly continued, "but

we're allowed to furnish our apartments with our own things, except for the stove and refrigerator. My only regret is that I didn't move out there the day after Mr. Farney passed!"

Mary Martha smiled. She never had owned the house she lived in, anyway—no matter what the deed claimed—and few of the furnishings were hers. Everything belonged to Mother Sims.

"If we don't forgive those who trespass against us, God won't forgive us," the pastor had warned in his sermon just last Sunday. She had tried to forgive. She no longer hated Mother Sims, and she had cared for her faithfully those last years after her stroke.

She still had some bitter memories, but she supposed she would have to lose her mind completely to forget those. Long ago she had resigned herself to her jaybird existence in someone else's nest, just as she had resigned herself to living in Parker's shadow. *I married him—and his mother,* she thought wryly. But she had been determined to see it through, no matter how completely that shadow shut out the sun.

Suddenly, Charlene Justice came into her mind, with her suggestions about "brightening up" the house. Mary Martha knew, though, that it would take much more than windows and skylights, even more than a bright sunny deck filled with flowers to brighten up that old house.

"I know you aren't listening to me," Dolly said with a resigned sigh. "But you'd like the Senior Center, Mary Martha. I know you would."

"You make it sound very attractive, Dolly," she answered. "Someday I may just surprise you."

"Yeah, yeah, and I may run for president," Dolly said. "I do want you to come to our Christmas luncheon day after tomorrow. While you're there, you can come up and see my apartment."

"I've seen your apartment, Dolly."

"I know, but you haven't seen the new drapes and bedspread my son got me for Christmas. You've got to see them! All shades of purple."

"Why am I not surprised?" Mary Martha murmured.

"My son would be glad to pick you up," Dolly offered.

"I'll tell you what," Mary Martha said, laughing, "if you will let Jayne do your hair next time, I'll come to your luncheon."

"It's a deal," Dolly agreed, throwing her a high five.

Chapter 8

Charlie Justice drove slowly down Main Street in the little town of Progress. She was early for her assignment to cover the luncheon at the Senior Citizens' Center. Rick thought the innovative home for the elderly would make a good Christmas feature story since there was no place quite like it in Olde Towne, or any of the neighboring towns.

"Get lots of photographs!" he had reminded her.

The Senior Center, she recalled from her preliminary research, had been built by a group of doctors seeking a tax break. Then it had been opened up to other investors. Now it was run by a board consisting of representatives of all concerned, including the residents. The one- and two-bedroom apartments—some rented, some purchased like condos—were a bit pricey, but that didn't seem to keep people away. The waiting list was extensive.

Charlie understood that the place was nothing like the typical "rest home," where residents languished in wheelchairs or shuffled listlessly up and down halls that smelled like disinfectant. The residents of the Senior Center were said to be active and happy.

Charlie stopped at the lone stoplight and looked around, taking in the old-fashioned attempts at honoring the season. She didn't care much for the candy canes on the light posts, but the posts themselves were beautiful wrought iron structures dripping clusters of round, white globes. They reminded her of paintings she had seen of lamplighters igniting the gaslights along tree-lined streets.

In Olde Towne, all the original trees had been replaced with dwarf specimens that were neater and more uniform. They lined up like obedient soldiers between the efficient modern lighting. *Everybody has air-conditioning now*, she thought. *There's no need for shade trees. I'll bet these giant maples and oaks are gorgeous in the fall, though.* They were beautiful even without leaves, their dark branches etched against the gray winter sky.

The light changed, and she moved on, trying to

escape the heavy nostalgia that had settled over her. "O little town of Progress," she sang, "how still we see thee lie!" *You've been lying here asleep since you were built back in the early 1900s,* she thought. It was a pretty little old-fashioned village, but she preferred the busy, hectic pace of their more modern town.

The Mayor's Ball had been exciting, and except for one near fainting spell that came on when she, luckily, was near the restroom, she had enjoyed it. She was glad Rick had insisted that they attend. They were carving out a niche for themselves in Olde Towne.

To her right, she noticed the building that housed the town's only newspaper, a weekly. "THE PROGRESS, ESTABLISHED 1892," proclaimed the dignified gold lettering on its double doors.

What would it be like to have only one edition to publish each week? she wondered. The news wouldn't be as fresh, but the pace certainly would be more leisurely than the one she and Rick and their small crew struggled with each day. She imagined having days instead of hours to prepare a feature story, having the luxury of reading it over one last time.

Rick planned to buy the weekly in Olde Towne as soon as they had the money, but working it into their already overextended schedule certainly would not make their lives more leisurely. She couldn't blame Rick, though. It was what they had planned when they came to Olde Towne. Of course, they had not planned on a baby coming along.

A wave of nausea washed over her, and she pulled the car over to the curb and sat with her head down against the steering wheel until it passed. *I have to see the doctor,* she thought. *What if something is wrong with the baby? And I must find a way to tell Rick.* Right now, though, she had to cover the luncheon, and she really needed something to abate her nausea. Just down the block, she had noticed a pharmacy. Maybe the pharmacist could give her something. She took the keys from the ignition, got out of the car, and locked the door.

Quickly, she retraced her route back to Hanley's Drugstore, climbed the two steps, and went inside. *I might as well be stepping back a hundred years,* she marveled, crossing the polished wooden floor to where a middle-aged man in a cream-colored pharmacist's coat stood behind a wooden counter.

"Do you have something I can take for nausea?" she asked in a low voice, conscious of a couple seated at a small round table down front.

The man studied her for a moment, then, also in a low voice, asked, "Are you pregnant, ma'am? I can't give you anything without a prescription if you are. I'm sorry, but it could harm the baby."

"All right," she answered, feeling a flush creep over her face as the couple turned to stare. She felt sure they thought she was trying to get something illegal. "Thanks, anyway," she murmured, turning and leaving the store, her heels clicking on the old wooden floor.

Still burning with embarrassment, she got back in the car and drove straight to the Senior Citizens' Center. She parked in the parking lot out front, slung her shoulder bag over her shoulder, and picked up the camera. She adjusted the waistband of her pantsuit. *Surely my clothes aren't getting tight already!* she thought in horror, fighting off another wave of nausea. She would get through this luncheon some way, then she would go home, call the doctor, and tell Rick.

As she entered the building's festive dining room, crowded with residents and guests, she saw Mary Martha Sims eating at a small table across from a large woman with purple hair. She decided to go over and speak to her before looking up the Senior Center's director, who was expecting her.

"Why, Charlene! What are you doing at a senior citizens' luncheon?" Mary Martha said with surprise.

"I'm doing a feature for the paper," she explained.

"But I didn't expect to find you here!"

"Oh, I'm just visiting a friend. Dolly, this is Charlene—" she began, then stopped.

"Charlie Justice," Charlie said, sticking out her hand. "I'm with *The Chronicle* over at Olde Towne."

"Charlene," Mary Martha said firmly to the purple-haired woman, "is the young woman who answered my ad about the dining room suite the other day. Charlene, this is my friend, Dolly Farney. At least I can remember her name!"

"Nice to meet you," Dolly said, shaking her hand.

"I've done some measuring, Mrs. Sims," Charlie said then, "but I—"

"—you would like to see it again before you make up your mind," Mary Martha finished for her.

It wasn't what she had intended to say, but Charlie let it pass. "I'll see you in a few minutes," she promised. "I've got to do some interviewing, take some photos. Here, you two go first." She raised the camera and snapped a picture of the two women. Then she turned and wandered through the big room taking shots of the huge Christmas tree and seasonal decorations, as well as random shots of the animated diners.

When she came back to the table, she sat down between the women and took her pen and notepad from her purse. "Would you like to tell me how you like living here at the Senior Center, Mrs. Farney?" she asked.

Dolly smiled broadly and began to sing the Senior Center's praises, as she so often had to Mary Martha.

"May I quote you, Mrs. Farney?" Charlie asked as the director led her off on a tour of the facility. When they returned, Mary Martha and Dolly were just finishing dessert.

"If you need to see the dining room suite again, why don't you just drive Mary Martha home?" Dolly suggested. "My son brought her, but he had to leave. She was going to call a cab."

"Why, I'd be glad to," Charlie agreed, relieved that her assignment was finished for now and she hadn't fainted or been sick.

Back at the Sims house, Charlie parked and went around to help her passenger out of the car.

"I've been hoping you would come back," Mary Martha said, leading the way inside and back to the dining room. "The table is large—it seats twelve—but you know that wide middle leaf can be removed."

"It really is exquisite!" Charlie breathed. "That's the only word for it!" Then she reached out to steady herself against the table as a wave of nausea swept over her.

"Oh, dear," Mary Martha said, pulling one of the

heavy chairs out from under the table. "Sit here and put your head down."

Charlie sank onto the chair and put her head between her knees. Once the spell had passed, she raised her head. "I'm so sorry!" she said. "You must think I'm a real wimp!"

Mary Martha chuckled. "I know exactly how you feel," she assured her. "Come back to the kitchen and rest for a few minutes. I think we both could do with a good hot cup of tea." She busied herself with the kettle and stove burner. "Have you had lunch? Can I get you something to eat?"

"Oh, no, Mrs. Sims, tea will be fine," Charlie answered, heading straight for Granny's rocker. "This is the most comfortable chair!" she said, rocking gently back and forth.

"That one's held many a mother and baby," Mary Martha said.

The comfortable silence lasted until the kettle whistled and Mary Martha filled two cups with tea. "Is your husband excited about being a father?" she asked, handing Charlie one cup on its saucer.

Charlie looked at her miserably, then dropped her gaze to the cup in her hands. "Mrs. Sims," she confessed, "I haven't even told him yet."

"Oh, my dear, you must tell him! Let him share the joy." Parker hadn't shared her joy over any of their expected babies or her pain when the last one had died. But she saw no reason to go into all that.

"We had such plans!" Charlie blurted. "We have such a tight schedule with the newspaper, and the town house we purchased isn't nearly big enough. There's no room in either of them for a baby. This wasn't supposed to happen, not yet, anyway!"

"Well, babies have a way of choosing their own time," Mary Martha pointed out. "Of course, people have more control over that now than we did in our day."

"That's my fault, Mrs. Sims," Charlie admitted. "I just got so busy I was careless. I'm so afraid of what Rick will say when he finds out. I'm worried that he might even leave me!"

"Oh, pshaw!" Mary Martha snorted. "You love each other, don't you? He won't leave." If Parker hadn't left her. . .but Parker was committed to his image, and divorce wasn't part of it. She reached over and patted Charlene on the shoulder. "Just trust in the Lord, dear," she advised. "He's never let me down."

Charlie ignored that. "I realize this is Rick's responsibility, too, but he's just finishing his master's, and he has plans to buy another paper, a weekly," she said. "We can't afford to hire more help or buy a bigger place to live. We can barely afford this dining room set, and we certainly have no room for both it and all the things a baby requires."

"Tell your husband," Mary Martha urged, "and let him help you make plans. It's his baby, too, though men usually don't recognize that fact until they hold the squirming little bundle in their arms."

Charlie smiled up at her. "I guess you're right. I know you are." She took a deep breath. "I need to get back to the office so I can get away early and get ready for the big announcement. I'll let you know how it goes and what we're going to do about that beautiful cherry dining set." She got up, placed her cup and saucer on the counter, and headed down the hall.

At the door, she turned suddenly and hugged Mary Martha. "Thank you!" she whispered, tears glistening in her eyes. Then she was out the door and getting into her car. She looked back and waved as she pulled away from the curb.

Chapter 9

Mary Martha stood on the stoop, fighting tears of her own. *What is wrong with me, spilling emotions all over the place?* she scolded. She supposed it was just that it had been a long time since she had seen Olivia, and talking with Charlene about her baby made her realize that she would never share that joy with her own daughter.

P.T.'s daughter and her children always spent more time with Eleanor's mother than they had with Mary Martha. She recalled her small granddaughter telling her one day, "I like you, Grandma, but I don't like this spooky old house. Something is always watching me!"

I hope Charlene will bring the baby by to visit sometime, she thought wistfully, watching a blue sedan pull to the curb and a man get out. Then she recognized the

Realtor who had been so set on selling her house the other night at the church. She turned to go back inside.

"Mrs. Sims! Mrs. Sims! Wait!" he called, running toward her. "I've got a buyer for your house!"

Mary Martha gave him her "no more nonsense" look, but it didn't work. Tom Winters held up one hand in a plea for patience while he caught his breath.

"It's a great offer!" he panted, and named a figure that would have widened Mary Martha's eyes had she not trained herself so well at hiding her feelings. It seemed to her a most generous sum, though she was sure P.T. would say it was too low. He and Parker were the money managers. She knew very little about property values.

I don't need that much money, she thought. She had no debts. The house was paid for years ago. Her income from Parker's pension at the bank and her social security was adequate to pay for her homeowner's insurance, property taxes, utilities, and what little food, medicine, and other necessities she bought. *Of course, I could give P.T. a third of it, set up a trust fund for Olivia in case she ever decides to leave the convent, and use my share to pay for an apartment at the Senior Center,* she mused.

Mary Martha banished the plan before it could settle in her mind. Parker would have been outraged at the mere thought of selling the Sims house!

"Mr. Winters, I've told you I am not interested," she said. "What part of that do you *not* understand?"

"But, Mrs. Sims," he protested, "it's such a good offer!"

"There is no good offer, sir, if one does not wish to sell," she said firmly, going into the house and closing the door in his face. She hated to be rude, but the man was as persistent as a cocklebur and just about as irritating! *If I wanted to sell, I'd find some other Realtor!* she thought, watching through the etched tulip in the door glass as Winters turned and walked dejectedly back to his car.

I can't believe how forceful I've become, she thought. *Coaching Charlene in her marriage relationship, sending Winters packing! Dolly certainly has been good for me in that respect.*

What is Dolly doing right now in her cheerful little apartment or down in the common areas where the residents enjoy each other's company? she wondered, walking through the silent, ghost-filled house.

Oh, she didn't believe in haunting spirits, but the house was full of ghosts, just the same. There was Mother Sims forever watching every move she made, even with her portrait stored in the attic. And there was the autocratic Parker, always in agreement with his mother, telling her what she could and could not do.

She recalled the time she had asked him if she could take a part-time job at Hanley's Drugstore—just a few hours each day while the children were at school. His angry response surprised her. "Why would you want to shame me like that? Isn't the allowance I give you enough to spend on frivolous things?" She had to admit that Parker never refused to buy anything she or the children needed, but it really hadn't been about money. She had simply wanted a little something of her own. Nevertheless, she had accepted his decree without argument.

Mary Martha fixed a fresh cup of tea and sat down with it at the small walnut table under the kitchen window. Looking out over the winter garden, she noticed that all was not brown. A fat little chipmunk scurried from its nest under the fountain to the back fence, where the burning bushes painted a deep swath of scarlet across the dark green of the evergreens. The crab apple tree in the center of the yard still held some of its small red fruit, and the hollies were filled with red berries.

Red and green for Christmas, she thought, glancing at the calendar. Only a handful of days remained before the holiday, but she thought she was ready. She re-checked the to-do list in her mind.

She had sent Christmas cards with checks in them to her granddaughter and all the great-grandchildren, who had matured beyond her ability to choose gifts for them. She had ordered a country ham, baked and sliced, for P.T. and Eleanor. She had contributed to the gift fund at church for the pastor and his wife. She had cards with cash in them ready for her hairdresser, the papergirl, and the—what was she supposed to call him now?—the letter carrier.

After Mother Sims had her stroke, Mary Martha had learned to bake the crusty loaves of cinnamon raisin bread they traditionally had given to service people and neighbors. Those neighbors had been gone for years now, though, and she hadn't baked Christmas loaves for at least a decade.

I'm as ready for Christmas as I will ever be, she thought with satisfaction, sipping her tea.

Then she remembered the big grapevine wreath Olivia had made for her in that craft class she took the last year before she went into the convent. Originally, the wreath had held real pinecones, English walnut shells, and bright-colored Indian corn. But when she brought it down from the attic to hang the next year, she found that a mouse had feasted on the corn. Mary Martha had replaced the naked white cobs with artificial holly. Every year since, she had hung the wreath, feeling, somehow, that it gave her a connection with her absent daughter.

Mary Martha knew she would have to subject her arthritic knees and hips to the climb up both long flights of steps to the attic. But she felt it was important to hang the wreath to remember Olivia and to honor the Savior's birth.

She rarely climbed the stairs anymore. After Parker's death, she had asked Ben and his sons to move her bedroom into Mother Sims's front parlor downstairs. She only entered the four upstairs rooms once a year when she called in the cleaning people.

Mary Martha got up, rinsed her cup, turned it upside down in the dish drainer, and headed for the stairway that wound up from the front hall.

I might as well get it done, she thought, placing her foot carefully on the first step and holding tightly to the polished walnut banister. She had fallen more than once on these stairs, so far without major injury, but she didn't want to risk a broken bone or worse, especially during the holidays.

Not that Christmas is so important anymore, she

thought, *except for what it represents*. Mary Martha stopped to catch her breath at the second-floor landing. Other than her Christmas Day visit with P.T.'s family, she would spend most of the holidays by herself here in this lonely old house.

Opening the door to the attic stairs, she started to climb the narrow risers, running her hand along the wall for support, since there was no railing here. At last, she was at the top. She took the green garbage bag she had tied around the wreath and turned to retrace her steps to the lower floors.

So far, so good! she thought as she shut the attic stair door and began the easier descent to the first floor. She couldn't see the steps now with the bag in her right hand and her left stretched out to slide along the banister.

She knew the minute she missed the step halfway down, but there was nothing she could do about it. The last thing she remembered was the frantic flailing of her arms and legs and one desperate prayer, "God, help me!"

Chapter 10

Charlie Justice sat on the raised hearth staring into the flames of the gas logs, wishing the ordeal ahead of her was over. She counted as the church bells down the street chimed the hour. Any minute now, Rick would come through that door.

What was she going to say? How could she tell him their dreams must be put on hold, maybe abandoned altogether? How could she destroy his well-laid plans? Right or wrong, he had left birth control up to her, and she had failed. Now they would both suffer the consequences.

She got up, walked restlessly to the window, and stood watching the beginnings of snow swirl around the light outside. *Maybe we'll have a white Christmas after all,* she thought. It was too early, though. Any snow that came now would be dirty slush by Christmas Day.

We really ought to get the tree up if we're going to have one, she thought. She felt better this evening, with no nausea and no faintness. Maybe they would go get a tree. It was their first Christmas in their new home. They really should have one.

I want a real one, she thought, *like we always had at the farm.* She remembered the whole family following Dad into the woods to find and cut the perfect tree. Those days were gone, but she had seen that a local club was selling evergreens in the bank's parking lot.

Where had she put that box of decorations—the one they had brought from the apartment in Lexington? Before they moved, she had carefully packed the treasures from her childhood and Rick's, too. She had also included a few new things they had purchased together. She felt sure the box was on that big shelf in the bedroom closet. She would ask Rick to get them down when he came.

Will that be before or after you drop your little bombshell? she asked herself, going to the refrigerator and pouring a glass of orange juice. Since she had been pregnant—there, she had said it!—she hadn't been able to stand the thought of cola. It was a wonder Rick hadn't noticed. It had always been her custom to begin the day with a Coke or Pepsi. Now she drank orange juice, tea, or milk, and she didn't even like milk! The baby was already running her life.

How am I going to tell him? she thought again. She wished she had brought Mrs. Sims's rocking chair home with her. Then she could sit there knitting little booties to ease him into her news. "If I could knit," she added sarcastically.

Hearing Rick's key in the lock, she set the orange juice on the counter and hurried back to the fireplace, her heart pounding in her throat. Her head began to spin, and she dropped quickly to her former seat on the hearth.

"I'm home, Toots!" he called. "Come see what I've got!"

"In here, Rick," she said, afraid to stand. But as he came into the room, she rose to her feet quickly, surprise covering her face.

"It's some kind of fir, like we used to have back home in Philadelphia. I'd forgotten how good they smell," Rick said, standing the small evergreen tree up on end. He was looking at the tree as her words came pouring out.

"Rick, we're—I'm going to have a baby," she blurted as she burst into tears and covered her eyes with both hands to shut out the frozen look on his face.

She heard the tree hit the floor with a thump, but except for the hissing of the flames beside her, there was no other sound. At least she hadn't heard the door open and shut, so apparently he was still standing there.

Finally, he cleared his throat. "You're having a baby," he repeated. It was a flat statement, not a question.

Charlie knew he was trying to come to terms with her startling announcement. She couldn't blame him for that. Her own acceptance of the fact had been a battle. She removed her hands from her eyes and looked up at him, but he was staring out the window, his back to her. The silence grew until she felt she couldn't stand it any longer.

"I'm so sorry, Rick!" she sobbed. "I didn't mean for it to happen. I just—"

She could sense the effort he was making to adjust to her news. Finally, he turned and crossed the space between them and pulled her up from the hearth and into his arms. He held her against his chest for a few moments until her sobs eased into a quiet sniffling. Then he let her go, just enough to brush the tears from her face with the tips of his fingers.

"Well, Toots, there's no need to cry," he said. "We're having a baby, and that's that. We'll just have to 'drop back and punt,' as my old football coach used to say. You'll need a lighter schedule at the paper, and I guess we'll need to rethink our plans to buy that weekly. Our baby must come first. Is it a 'he' or a 'she'? What does the doctor say?"

"I don't know what it is, Rick," she answered. "I haven't even been to the doctor, yet. But I've taken the test three times, and it is definitely positive. Then there's the nausea and fainting."

Rick drew her close again. "I'm so sorry, Charlie," he whispered into her hair. "You've been miserable, and I've been too self-absorbed to notice."

"You told me from the beginning to make sure we didn't start a family until we were ready!" she cried. "Now all our plans are ruined. Rick, I wouldn't blame you if you walked out," she choked, the tears beginning to overflow again.

"Out?" he repeated. "What are you talking about? We're having a baby. It's mine, too, you know. It's not what I wanted at this stage of the game, but we'll just have to deal with it—together."

Relief swept over her. He was reacting just like Mrs. Sims had said he would. Suddenly, she remembered the dining room suite. "We don't have room here for a baby, Rick, even if we don't buy Mrs. Sims's dining room suite."

He looked around critically. "This open area between the living room and the kitchen is not a good place for a baby's room," he agreed. "There's no way to shut out noise, no way to hide—whatever it is babies need that should be hidden—diaper holders and whatever," he finished lamely. "I suppose we could squeeze a baby bed into our bedroom, but our so-called master bathroom probably won't accommodate even an extra can of baby powder. What do they put on babies nowadays?"

"Rick, what are we going to do?" she asked, swiping impatiently at the tears that wouldn't stop now that they had started.

"Hey, Toots," he admonished, "no more tears! We'll just have to cope until we can sell this place and find something bigger that we can afford. How long before the baby gets here?"

"Maybe seven months," she answered.

"Well, he—or she—can camp out in our bedroom for a while. We'll work it out, sweetheart," he assured her. Then he grinned, and she was glad to see the grin travel upward to sparkle in his eyes. "It might have helped, though, if I'd caught you reading Dr. Spock or knitting baby things. I might have been a little better prepared for your news."

"I thought about it," she grinned back, "but I can't

knit, for one thing, and my sister never used Spock. She's always depended on Dr. James Dobson as her guide in raising children."

"Call your sister," he suggested. "Call Dr. Dobson! We're going to need all the help we can get."

"I'll call Mrs. Sims first and tell her we won't be taking the dining room set," she said, moving toward the phone.

"Charlie, wait. Let's buy the dining room set," he said eagerly. "Let's go on with our plans to entertain. And how about calling my folks and have them come for Christmas dinner so we can make the big announcement. They'll be so excited!"

"But, Rick, where would we put them?" she protested, panic rising at the thought of his parents so closely underfoot while she tried to cope with nausea and all the needs at the paper.

"Charlie, they can afford to stay at the hotel. They won't mind. I'm their only hope for grandchildren, you know."

She leaned against him. "I love you, Richard Justice," she whispered.

"I love you, too," he answered. "Now pick up that phone and tell Mrs. Sims we'll take that dining room set. It will fit, won't it?"

"All but the china cabinet," she said, "but we don't need it."

"Call her!" he insisted.

She got the ad from her purse, picked up the phone, and punched in the numbers. Finally, she hung up. "There's no answer," she informed him.

"It can wait," he said. "Let's decorate this Christmas tree. Then we'll have some eggnog while we admire it."

Her stomach rolled at the thought of eggnog. "Maybe some popcorn," she suggested. "We don't have any eggnog, but I'm pretty sure the ornaments are on that top shelf in the upstairs closet."

As he took the stairs two at a time, she dialed Mrs. Sims's number again, hearing it ring and ring without answer. *Where can she be?* Charlie wondered. "I hope nothing has happened to Mrs. Sims," she told Rick. "She's more than eighty years old and living in that old house alone."

Maybe she's visiting Dolly Farney, she told herself, *or her son.* Charlie thought she recalled Mrs. Sims saying she had a son. *I'll try again later,* she promised, turning to explore the box of decorations Rick had set on the hearth. She was so happy to be here with him, getting ready to decorate their Christmas tree, looking forward to the holidays together.

Chapter 11

Mary Martha Sims could hear the phone ringing in the kitchen, but she couldn't get up from where she lay at the foot of the stairs. Excruciating pain shot through her left hip when she tried to move, and her head throbbed mercilessly.

"What a stupid thing to do!" she scolded aloud. If only she had held more tightly to the banister, been less careless about where she placed her foot, the accident might have been averted. But Mary Martha knew it would do no good to keep going over it in her mind. She was in serious trouble—alone, no way to reach a phone. She folded her arm to cradle her aching head, knowing it might be days before anyone thought to check on her.

What day is it? she wondered. The pastor's wife

wouldn't come until next Tuesday to take her to Kroger's. Meanwhile, if she didn't show up at church on Sunday morning, Dolly might try to reach her. Dolly didn't come every Sunday, though. Sometimes, she went with her son to his church. P.T. would call on Sunday afternoon. That was a sure thing, and when she didn't answer the phone, surely he would come to check on her. How many hours of pain and helplessness lay between now and then?

"Mother Sims, I'm so sorry P.T. slid down the banister and fell into your Grecian urn. Yes, I know it cannot be replaced, but aren't you glad he wasn't hurt? Just that little cut on his chin." She held out her hands in a plea for understanding. *"He's just a little boy! He needs space. He needs to be able to make noise sometimes. And Olivia needs to have friends over once in a while. Please, Mother Sims!"*

I must have passed out, she thought, hearing the phone ringing again. She had to get to it! But when she tried to move, the intense pain in her hip made her cry out. Then she felt the blackness closing over her again.

"Parker," she said, *"could we please have a home of our own? It wouldn't have to be new or fancy—just a little cottage somewhere, just us and the children."*

She knew the answer before she heard his words. "This is our home, Mary Martha. My grandfather built this house. It is my heritage. It is our children's heritage."

"But, Parker," she pleaded, "our children need a place to run and play. Our little boy needs a fenced-in yard where he can have a puppy. Our little girl needs a place to have tea parties with her friends. I need a kitchen where I can make cookies and pot flowers for the windowsill!"

"What is wrong with you?" Parker asked angrily. "We have a lovely home here. Mother has bent over backwards to make us welcome, to see that we are well-fed and comfortable."

"I can't live like this anymore," she burst out, "with the unreasonable restraints and those condemning eyes watching everything the children and I do! Please, Parker!"

She flinched at the narrowing of his eyes, though he had never actually hit her. "You are my wife, Mary Martha," he said coldly. "You will do as I say. And you will not be rude or ungrateful to my mother."

She knew that was his final answer.

The phone was ringing again. She had to answer it. Parker would be furious if he missed a business call because of her neglect. She tried to get up, then fell back before the fierce onslaught of pain. This time she welcomed the blackness.

Chapter 12

"I t's nearly ten o'clock, Rick, and Mrs. Sims still isn't answering her phone," Charlie said. "I'm worried about her."

"Do you want me to drive you over there to check on her?" he offered. "I don't think you should go alone. If something is wrong, you could need help."

She didn't argue. Grabbing her jacket, she followed him out to the five-year-old gray Chrysler Rick's father had passed on to them when he bought his new one. She got in on the passenger's side and fastened the seat belt.

"I can't imagine where she could be," Charlie worried as Rick drove the fifteen miles from Olde Towne to Progress. "I'm so afraid she's had a stroke or a heart attack or maybe a fall down those steep, dark stairs."

"Don't borrow trouble, Charlie," he advised. "Maybe

she fell asleep and didn't hear the phone. You said she's over eighty. Maybe her hearing isn't so good."

"It seemed fine to me. But she's frail. I'll bet she doesn't weigh ninety pounds. She's bright, though. I really like her, Rick."

"I'm looking forward to meeting her," he said, stopping for the stoplight in Progress.

"Turn left at that next street," Charlie directed. "It's just a few blocks down that way, on the left."

When Rick pulled to the curb in front of the familiar brick house, Charlie hurried out of the car and up the walk. She twisted the old-fashioned doorbell and heard it shrill through the house. "Mrs. Sims!" she called. "Mrs. Sims, are you here? It's Charlie—Charlene!" She listened hopefully for a response but heard nothing except the distant sound of traffic and, a few blocks over, the frenzied barking of a dog. The light was on in the hall, and she bent to peer through the clear spaces of the etched tulip in the front door.

"Oh, Rick!" she cried. "Call 911! She's there on the floor at the foot of the stairs! She's not moving!" She turned the doorknob and pushed against it, but the locked door was thick and strong. She heard Rick talking into his cell phone, asking for an ambulance, giving the address. "Mrs. Sims!" she called again. "Can you hear me? Hang on! We're getting help."

Charlie knew it couldn't have been more than a few minutes before the ambulance came screaming down the street, lights flashing. But it seemed like hours as she stood there praying for some sign of life from the small, crumpled heap beyond the locked door.

Was I praying? she wondered in amazement. Charlie hadn't prayed in years! She had tossed faith into a closet with other outgrown childhood fantasies—Santa Claus, the Easter Bunny, the Tooth Fairy. Like the modern young woman she was, Charlie had learned to depend on her own wits and strength. At this moment, though, she knew they were hopelessly inadequate. She needed something—Someone—more powerful than she was.

Two uniformed EMTs rushed onto the stoop. "Stand back, ma'am, while we open this door," one of them warned. Then they had the door open and were kneeling over the small, still figure.

"I've got a pulse!" one of them exclaimed. "Let's get her out of here!"

Charlie's breath caught on a sob of relief as she watched the men wheel Mrs. Sims out of the house and lift her into the ambulance. Her head began to swim, and she clutched her husband's arm, but she refused to faint. "I'm going with her," she said so firmly that no one argued with her, not even Rick.

"I'll follow in the car," he said.

Then she was in the ambulance, holding Mrs. Sims's limp hand, pleading silently but earnestly with God for the old woman's life. "I've been arrogant and foolish!" she confessed. "I wouldn't blame you for writing me off, but Mrs. Sims trusts in You. She told me that You have never let her down."

Charlie swiped futilely at the tears running down her cheeks. "Please, God, don't let her down now!" she begged as the ambulance pulled up to the hospital's emergency entrance and the EMTs whisked Mrs. Sims inside.

Chapter 13

M ary Martha Sims opened her eyes and looked around. "Where am I?" she asked. Then, if her head hadn't hurt so badly, she would have laughed. Wasn't that the classic line of every fainting movie heroine since silent films?

Had she simply fainted? No, she remembered now. She had fallen down the stairs and passed out from the pain. She struggled to see her legs. She was sure she had broken something, probably her hip. That was where the terrible pain had been. It didn't hurt so badly now. Maybe she was drifting on some cloud of medication.

Judging by all the tubes and monitors, I must be in the hospital, Mary Martha thought, *but how did I get here? How on earth did anyone know I was lying there at the foot of the stairs? Did the good Lord send an angel to rescue me?*

"It's about time you woke up," Charlie said, coming into the room. "How do you feel?"

"I've felt better," Mary Martha responded wryly. "How did I get here?"

"I kept trying to call you about the dining room suite. When you didn't answer, Rick and I drove over to check on you," she explained. "When I saw you lying in a heap on the floor, we called 911."

"So you're the angel!" Mary Martha said with a weak grin, sinking back against the pillows. "Has anyone called P.T.? Don't bother calling Olivia. It's so hard for her to get away. I'll tell her about it later."

"Your son is on his way," Rick said, joining them. "I'm Rick Justice," he added, "and I'm very glad to meet you, Mrs. Sims."

Mary Martha threw a questioning glance at Charlie and received a reassuring smile in return. Then it came to her. *Charlene must have told him about the baby,* she thought. *I knew it would be all right.* "I'm glad to meet you, too, Mr. Justice. I've heard a lot about you," she said.

"I'll bet you have," he said with a grin, "but I promise to do better."

"Out! Out! Out!" a nurse commanded, bustling around the bed, straightening covers and plumping pillows. "This lady just came back from hip surgery. She doesn't need company! You can come back in the morning."

"Go on," Mary Martha said. "I'll be okay. Thank you so much for rescuing me. I thought I might lie there for hours, maybe even days, but I should have had more faith." She wanted to say more, but her eyes just wouldn't stay open. "Call Dolly," she managed to get out before sleep took over.

She didn't even know when Charlie and Rick left, or when P.T. and Eleanor arrived. She thought she heard the nurse say, "I'll call you if she needs you."

I don't need anybody or anything, she thought, floating in a euphoria of warmth and love. "The eternal God is my refuge," she murmured, "and underneath are the everlasting arms."

Chapter 14

Charlie Justice, holding a magazine and a small pot of pink azaleas, stopped just outside the closed door of the hospital room.

"No, ma'am, you cannot go home by yourself," she heard the doctor say emphatically.

"I will not impose upon my son and daughter-in-law or anybody else for that matter," she heard Mrs. Sims answer just as emphatically.

"Then you will have to go into an extended care facility until you're able to wait on yourself. It could take six to eight weeks, and then you may still have to walk with a walker or a three-pronged cane. You had a clean break, but at your age, Mrs. Sims—"

"I know, doctor," Mary Martha broke in, "old bones take longer to heal."

"Exactly!" the doctor said with a laugh.

I wish I could take care of her, Charlie thought, surprised at the depth of her feelings. She knew, though, with her schedule at the paper, it was impossible. *Maybe I could stay with her at night and someone else could take the day shift,* she thought.

That would leave Rick alone at night, and evening was about the only time they had together, with their scattered work assignments. Of course, he could come with her, but she doubted that he would want to take on the extra commuting between the towns. Still, she hated to think of Mrs. Sims going to a nursing home.

"I can arrange for the Home Health people to come in once a day to help with baths and meals once you graduate to a walker," the doctor was saying. "Do you have to climb those stairs?"

"What are they talking about?" a voice asked beside her.

Charlie turned to see a plump woman she finally identified as Dolly Farney. Her hair was a dark silver now, the purple nearly gone.

"Mrs. Sims wants to go home, and the doctor is forbidding it," Charlie explained, still fascinated by the change in the woman's looks. "I like your hair," she said. "It's very becoming."

Dolly laughed. "I promised Mary Martha if she came to our luncheon, I would let her beautician do my hair. Mary Martha hates that purple." She chuckled, and Charlie smiled noncommittally. "The color is hard to control when you do it yourself," Dolly added. "I like this silver, though. I can't really afford it, but why not? 'I'm worth it!' " she said haughtily, in such a good imitation of the TV ad that Charlie laughed.

"Anyway, that's what I came to talk with her about," Dolly said, moving on into the room. "Mrs. Sims is going home with me, Doc," she said, "as soon as she can get in and out of bed without me lifting her."

"Dolly, I will not!" Charlie heard Mrs. Sims protest. "I just told this stubborn doctor that I will not impose on anybody. I took care of Mother Sims for several years after she had her stroke, and I know how hard it is to be the caregiver for an invalid."

Dolly snorted. "If you were as mean as that old woman, I wouldn't take you! By the way, how do you like my hair?"

Charlie saw Mrs. Sims eyes widen in disbelief. "It looks great!" she said. "Jayne did it, didn't she?"

Dolly nodded. "When can I take her home, Doc?" she asked.

"We can probably release her before Christmas Eve," he answered. "Nobody likes to hang around a hospital at Christmas."

"Dolly Farney, I am not going to spend two months cooped up in that little cracker box apartment of yours, with you having to wait on me hand and foot!" Mary Martha protested.

"*Hummph!* You are helpless and at my mercy," Dolly said. Then they both burst into giggles.

Just like two little girls, Charlie thought in amazement. It was a side of Mrs. Sims she had not seen, and she doubted that it was allowed to surface very often.

Apparently, Dolly was good for her. Didn't the Bible say something about laughter doing good like a medicine?

"You cranky old woman!" Dolly said, when she could stop laughing.

"You're older than I am!" Mary Martha snapped.

"But I'm not as cranky as you are," Dolly shot back at her. Then they went off into another spasm of giggles.

"Well, ladies, I'll leave you to settle this between you," the doctor said, backing toward the door. "Just remember, Mrs. Sims, you are not going home alone, and that's my final word on it." He turned quickly and left the room.

"She's going home with me, Doc," Dolly called after him.

"I am not!" Charlie thought Mrs. Sims would have stomped her foot if she could. "I am not sleeping with you in that little twin bed when I've got four big empty ones at home."

"Mary Martha Sims, I was planning to sleep on the couch!" Dolly said indignantly. Then she added, "But if you've got all those empty beds, then I'll just go home with you."

"And you'll be the next to fall down the stairs and break something," Mary Martha predicted. "All the beds but mine are upstairs."

"Mrs. Sims," Charlie broke in, "that sounds like a wonderful idea. Maybe Rick and your son could move a bed downstairs. There'll be plenty of room in the dining room when we take out the dining set. And I could come over and stay on Friday nights and Saturdays until I have to go in to work and help with the Sunday edition. That would give Mrs. Farney a chance to go home for a while. It's only for a couple of months."

"Sounds good to me," Dolly agreed eagerly. "How

about you, old cranky?" she asked.

Charlie saw Mrs. Sims take a deep breath. "Between the two of you, what choice do I have? But I always pay my way. I won't let either of you do it for nothing," she vowed.

"All right," Dolly agreed quickly. "You can pay Jayne to do my hair for the next two months."

"Gladly!" Mary Martha said. "I couldn't stand being waited on by a purple prune!"

Charlie laughed with them this time. "Well, I need to get back to the newspaper," she said, setting the magazine and the flowers on the bedside table. "Call me if the doctor dismisses you before I get back, and I'll drive you home."

"Thank you, dear," Mary Martha said, "but since I can't bend this monster of a cast, I don't think I could get into that little car of yours. I suppose I'll have to go back the way I came—in an ambulance."

Charlie nodded. "Then I'll follow you and make sure you're all settled in until Mrs. Farney gets there."

As she bent over the bed to give Mary Martha a hug, she was almost sure she saw a glimmer of tears in the woman's dark eyes. She swallowed the lump gathering in her own throat. *It's amazing how much*

I've come to care for this little old lady in such a short time! she thought.

Maybe I was meant to get to know Mrs. Sims, she thought as she left the hospital. *With my parents gone and Rick's so far away, our baby is going to need a grandmother.*

Chapter 15

There's been more laughter echoing through this empty old house in the few hours since Dolly's been here than it has known in all its history, Mary Martha Sims thought, carefully maneuvering herself and the burdensome cast from the bed to her new motorized wheelchair. And she certainly hadn't been lonely! *I almost miss the peaceful solitude,* she thought.

Dolly had been so good to come and stay with her. She couldn't imagine how she would have managed without her, and Charlene and Rick had become like her own children. Grandchildren, she supposed she should say. Or maybe great-grandchildren. She wasn't sure that either of them had turned thirty yet.

Soon I'll have a new little great-great-grandchild to rock in Granny's rocker, she thought as she wheeled herself down the hallway and into the kitchen.

"You're getting pretty good with that chariot," Dolly said when she saw her. "Are you ready for lunch? The pastor's wife brought us a pot of brown beans and a salad, and I've made some herb corn bread. A little sage and basil make all the difference." She opened the oven door and peeked inside. "It should be ready in about ten minutes."

"It smells wonderful!" Mary Martha said. "Why didn't Mrs. Tanner come in to see me?"

"You were asleep, and she didn't want to wake you," Dolly answered. "How's the pain?"

"Bearable. I'm not taking any more pain medication until bedtime," she added. "I have to taper off of the drugs sometime. Did Rick and P.T. get your bed moved down here okay?"

"Oh, yes, and a little chest of drawers to hold my things," Dolly said. "Since Charlie and Rick took that huge old dining room set, there's room for three beds in there!"

Mary Martha gave her friend a satisfied smile.

"You had a call about the piano, too," Dolly said. "A man's coming to look at it the day after Christmas," Dolly said, taking the pan of corn bread from the oven. "It's hard to believe it's Christmas Eve already!"

"I don't think I've ever had brown beans and corn bread on Christmas Eve," Mary Martha said.

"Well, it's time you lived a little, girl!" Dolly laughed. "Anyway, we've had turkey and all the trimmings twice this past week, and you'll probably have it again tomorrow at P.T.'s and Eleanor's."

"P.T. and Eleanor have a country ham. I sent it to them. There'll be oysters, too." Mary Martha shuddered. "I never touch those slimy things!"

"I like 'em scalloped," Dolly said, sliding corn bread onto one of Mother Sims's best dessert plates, "but I only eat the dressing around 'em. Bob and Peggy will have both ham and turkey and cranberry sauce made from scratch. What I'm looking forward to, though, is Peggy's jam cake with caramel icing so rich it'll curl your toes! Peggy's a good cook."

"Eleanor always has a raspberry trifle for dessert," Mary Martha said, "with real whipped cream to top it."

"Are the kids coming in this year?" Dolly asked, ladling beans into two of Mother Sims's best china bowls.

I'm not going to say a word, Mary Martha vowed. *If they get broken, they get broken. Who's left to care?*

"No, one of the great-grandchildren is expecting any minute, so none of them are making the trip," she answered. Dolly placed the bowls on two cheery Christmas placemats that had appeared on the small walnut table under the window.

"Both our grandsons are going to their wives' homes for Christmas," Dolly said, adding two small plates of congealed salad and a dish of green tomato relish to the table. "It will just be Bob and Peggy, Peggy's mother, and me this year. I'll be back over here early, probably before you get back. Do you think you can ride in P.T.'s car with that cast?"

"The backseat of that Lincoln has room for the kitchen sink if I wanted to take it!" Mary Martha said, easing her wheelchair under the table's raised leaf.

Mary Martha bowed her head while Dolly offered thanks. Then they ate hungrily and in silence for several minutes. Dinner was over, and the ladies were sipping their second cup of tea when the doorbell rang. Dolly went to answer it and came back followed by Charlie Justice.

"Merry Christmas, Mrs. Sims!" the young woman said, dropping a kiss on the top of her head. "I brought you two some pecan cake."

"Thank you, dear. Just put it on the counter," Mary Martha suggested, "and we'll eat it later. Right now we're full of beans!"

Charlie laughed. "You two are always full of beans!"

"And corn bread today," Dolly added, dumping dirty dishes into the sink.

Mary Martha's heart sank at the unmistakable sound of something breaking. "Oops!" Dolly said.

Mary Martha closed her eyes, waiting for the expected rebuke. Then, realizing that there was no one to give it, she grinned. "Merry Christmas, Mother Sims!" she said.

"I'm sorry," Dolly offered. "I think I can glue it back together."

"Throw it out," Mary Martha said. "There's plenty more where that came from. Would you like some beans and corn bread, Charlene?" she asked.

She was surprised to see the young woman turn pale and drop into the rocking chair.

"Oh, oh!" Dolly said. "Been there and done that!"

Chapter 16

Charlie Justice felt better now, but she stayed in the rocker, the spell of its ancient rhythm relaxing her taut nerves. She sensed the pleasant memories of mothers and babies past who had taken comfort from its soothing motion.

Suddenly, she felt a quickening inside her. She sat up and placed both feet firmly on the floor. *It can't be the baby!* she thought. *Too early for that!* Charlie sank back against the cushion. Her feet began to push against the floor, rocking the chair of their own volition, and she felt a warmth spreading through her. She knew her baby hadn't moved. But it was there, alive and growing, an infinitesimal but very real little person. Bemused, she looked up at Mary Martha, who was watching her with a soft, remembering smile.

"What did you say you want for this rocker?" Charlie asked.

"I've changed my mind about that," Mary Martha answered curtly. "I'm not going to sell Granny's rocker." She saw Charlie's eager expression melt into disappointment.

"Oh," she said. "Well, I can understand why you wouldn't want to part with it."

"I'm going to part with it," Mary Martha explained. "I'm just not going to sell it." She smiled. "It's yours, dear. I hope you and your little one will spend many happy hours in it."

"But, Mrs. Sims," Charlie began. "I can't—"

"I told you I always pay my way," Mary Martha interrupted. "Of course, its monetary value is little, but that chair is rich in love and tradition. I can't think of anyone I'd rather see have it than you."

"I'll help you get it into your car," Dolly offered. "Take it before the old grouch changes her mind!" she added, smiling fondly at Mary Martha.

A few minutes later, Mary Martha sat in her wheelchair on the front walk, watching her Granny's chair ride down the street under the tied-down trunk lid of Charlie's little white car.

Suddenly, she understood why Parker had felt so

strongly about the Sims house. *It had been his anchor to the world, his place mark in the epic of human life*, she thought, feeling a sharp twinge of loneliness as the chair disappeared around the corner.

She couldn't help feeling that some kind of progress had been made here this afternoon, though. She wasn't sure what it was. But at least she no longer felt guilty about getting rid of the things that had belonged to Mother Sims.

She turned quickly and looked at the house, as though fearing it had read her thoughts and would tattle. The house stared back—austere, forbidding. But Mary Martha realized with amazement that it no longer had any power over her, not even to make her feel bitter toward Mother Sims for her unrelenting oppression, not even toward Parker for making her live there all those years.

She moved slowly up the walk, steering the chair carefully around the sunken place. She supposed that she could live in the house for another sixty years without ever spending one comfortable day in it. Truthfully, it was just a dank, dark, old house filled with things that had outlasted those who valued them.

Dolly seems so comfortable in her nice little apartment down at the Senior Citizens' Center, she thought as her friend helped her maneuver the chair up onto the low stoop.

Mary Martha reached for the doorknob, then paused with her hand in midair. Parker never would have wanted her to sell the house.

She smiled, turned the knob, and wheeled into the dimness of the entry. *Parker is gone,* she thought, *and the house really is too big for me.*

About the Author

Wanda Luttrell was born and raised in Franklin County, Kentucky, where she lives with her husband, John. She is the mother of five grown children and was employed for nearly thirty years by the Kentucky Association of School Administrators.

Wanda's writing has appeared in various Christian and general publications. Her interest in local Kentucky history eventually led her to write several books with themes from the Bluegrass State, including *The Legacy of Drennan's Crossing*, *In the Shadow of the White Rose*, and the Sarah's Journey series.

A Letter to Our Readers

Dear Readers:

In order that we might better contribute to your reading enjoyment, we would appreciate your taking a few minutes to respond to the following questions. When completed, please return to the following: Fiction Editor, Barbour Publishing, Inc., P.O. Box 719, Uhrichsville, OH 44683.

1. Did you enjoy reading *Keeping Christmas*?
   ❑ Very much—I would like to see more books like this.
   ❑ Moderately—I would have enjoyed it more if _____
   _____
   _____

2. What influenced your decision to purchase this book?
   (Check those that apply.)
   ❑ Cover   ❑ Back cover copy   ❑ Title   ❑ Price
   ❑ Friends   ❑ Publicity   ❑ Other

3. Which story was your favorite?
   ❑ *No Holly, No Ivy*   ❑ *O Little Town of Progress*

4. Please check your age range:
   ❑ Under 18   ❑ 18–24   ❑ 25–34
   ❑ 35–45   ❑ 46–55   ❑ Over 55

5. How many hours per week do you read? _____

Name _____

Occupation _____

Address _____

City _____ State _____ Zip _____

E-mail _____

If you enjoyed

KEEPING
CHRISTMAS

then read:

ROOM AT THE INN

Love Checks Into Two
Christmas Novellas

Orange Blossom Christmas by Kristy Dykes
Mustangs and Mistletoe by Pamela Griffin

Available wherever books are sold.
Or order from:
Barbour Publishing, Inc.
P.O. Box 721
Uhrichsville, Ohio 44683
http://www.barbourbooks.com

You may order by mail for $4.97 and add $2.00 to your order for shipping.
Prices subject to change without notice.